THE GARGOYLE, THE NUTCRACKER, AND THE CHRISTMAS SPIRIT

THE GARGOYLE, THE NUTCRACKER, AND THE CHRISTMAS SPIRIT

MEGAN PARKER

Contents

Dedicated to my best friend, who didn't cringe when she read the very first draft of my prologue.

Prologue

He dashed into the rubble of the battlefield. He saw victory for his kingdom, and his own future laid out before him. As he blitzed past swinging swords and leaped over tumbled rocks and vines, he knew he had one shot to finish this.

His Commander yelled out to him, something he didn't hear. All he could hear was his heartbeat, his breath, a resounding yet steady drum in his chest.

From behind the evil King Micenor, he drew his sword. He leapt so high that he stood taller than the monstrous King. He didn't hesitate in slicing off all three heads of the Mouse King, for he knew what the aftermath was worth.

At least, that's how his father always told the story. Nedrall always remembered hearing his father's tale of victory so fondly.

Nedrall sat patiently on the couch as he looked at the hand-knitted, cranberry red rug that was stitched with details of a fine, young hero standing among his fellow soldiers. The light from the fire illuminated Ned's view, flickering as did his heavy eyelids. Behind him, he heard soft footsteps approaching. The sleepiness turned to excitement as Ned turned to see his father, A handsome older gentleman whose only flaw seemed to be a few scars here and there. Ned's father was charming, lean, and strong. Combed gray hair poked out of his face and head. He had donned his favorite cardigan in preparation for the special story he'd tell that night. His pajamas were a matching green and red plaid set that came with a loose button-up shirt and pants. Ned waited excitedly as his father sat in the wooden rocking chair across the living room. Ned scooted towards the edge of his seat, eager for tonight's bed-time story.

"Are you ready?" Said Ned's father in a quiet yet enthusiastic voice while picking up a book from the coffee table.

"Yeah!" Ned exclaimed, a smile spreading across both of their faces, as they both knew this story by heart.

"Alright then," Nedrall's father started. "Once upon a time, there lived an evil mouse king. He was one of many kings- there was the King of Takkochsivy, King Klaus, the evil king of the micenors, King Mouserinks, and the mysterious and secretive king of the gargoyles, King Khelbent. King Mouserinks of the Micenors had been King Klaus' enemy for generations, and King Khelbent sought magical power beyond your imagination- leading both of them to greed. The two kings planned an attack against King Klaus and his people."

Ned's grin grew wider. He liked this story so much because it was true.

"So, the General of Takkochsivy gathered an army unlike any other- they were fast, articulate, strong, skilled, and powerful. He waited for the perfect moment to strike- and strike he did! He defeated every last minion of the evil king Micerinks and slayed the king himself! The brave General saved his kingdom, his friends, his people, and his king. The end."

Ned's father peered over his book to make sure Ned was still paying attention. And he was- to every word.

Ned's father, General Navid Nutcracker, picked up his son and set him on his feet. Just as they were about to head on to bed, as was routine every night, Navid paused. He had a different idea.

"How about a new story tonight, yeah?" He presented the idea to Ned.

"Yes! New story!" Nedrall cheered, pumping his fist to the air.

"All right, all right, get settled in bed and I'll be right there."

Ned ran into his room, jumped onto his bed and hastily pulled the covers over his legs. By the time Navid entered the room, Ned was already eagerly waiting.

"You ready?" Navid asked, chuckling at his son's eagerness.

"Yes, yes, yes!" Ned urged him on.

"All right. Long, long ago- when the world was new- only magical spirits roamed the land. The Spirit of Winter, The descendants of the house of Klaus, the descendants of the house of Khelbent, and the descendants of the house of Mouserinks. Ring a bell?" Navid explained, taking a seat on the chair at Nedrall's desk.

"Those are all the kings! Wait, does that mean you defeated a magic spirit? That's so cool!" Ned leaned forward, gaining more interest by the second.

"Yes, King Mouserinks was the descendant of magical spirits." Navid told him. "The roots of all these magical spirits were created by the Winter Spirit, and all of them were powerful beings. To this day, no one has found the Winter Spirit. But rumors say that the Winter Spirit created another spirit the day I defeated King Mouserinks, though some people have claimed to see a glowing girl in the woods, no one has been able to prove that she exists."

"So our king is a magic spirit? What can he do? Can he shoot fireballs or move things with his mind? Oh! Can he make swords and bows and arrows out of thin air?" Ned asked eagerly, slicing an imaginary sword through the air.

"Not quite," Nedrall started. "He comes from magical ancestors. He is wise, and strong. He has magic stronger than fireballs and mind-magic."

"What magic does he have?" Ned asked, hoping very much that King Klaus had superpowers like those he read in comics.

"Knowledge and healing. They say he knows the recipe for an ancient magic tea that heals any illness or wound." Navid answered, appreciating the power more than Ned.

"That's it?" Ned asked disappointedly.

"I'm afraid so," Navid stood and leaned against the doorframe of Ned's room.

"What about the other spirits? Like the Winter Spirit and King Khelbent? What magic do they have?"

"Well, for starters, there's the King of gargoyles, King Khelbent. He's the one that can create weapons out of nothing, and his body is invulnerable to anything but magic." Navid's expression changed from one of interest to distrust. Ned picked up on this detail.

"Is he a bad guy?" Ned implored.

"Well, he doesn't like us, but I don't think that makes him a bad guy to us just yet." Navid shrugged. "King Klaus thinks he just wants more magic."

"Well, none of us are magical," Ned concluded.

Navid paused for a brief moment. "Indeed we aren't."

"If he wants magic, why doesn't he just ask the Winter Spirit for more?" Ned kept the questions coming.

"Well I don't think the Winter Spirit can do that, either that or it doesn't want to."

"Well why doesn't it want to?"

"The same reason I don't give you sugar after nine," Navid joked. "It's dangerous, and you probably won't stop until someone puts you down."

"What about the rumored spirit? The one that's been around since you defeated King Micerinks?" Ned pushed on.

"Well, lately, people have told me that they have seen a magical looking girl roaming the Cidarian Forest. They're calling her the Christmas Spirit, and they said she glows a warm glow, like the sun."

"Do ya think I can find her?" Ned questioned. "Did they say anything else about her?"

Navid, seeing the mistake he made in triggering his son's curiosity, sighed and rolled his head back. "I dunno Ned. But, I better not hear that you went into those woods looking for her, you understand?"

With his military background, Navid's commands sounded quite intimidating. But not to Ned. He was already scheming his plan to go into the Cidarian forest to find this spirit.

"I'm serious, Ned," Navid noticed his son's smug look. "It could be dangerous."

"I know, I know."

"Good. You're just ten years old, I can't have you runnin' around the woods by yourself."

"But is it okay if I go into town tomorrow with Charles before training?" Ned asked. "He has errands to run."

Navid sighed. "Sure, but I'd better not catch you in the woods."

"Yeah, yeah, I know." Ned slid deeper under his covers, waiting for his father to leave the room. As soon as he did, Ned zoomed to his desk, grabbed his walkie-talkie, and asked his friend to help him devise a plan to find the Christmas Spirit.

The next morning, Ned woke up before his father did. He jumped out of bed and quickly put on the warmest clothes in his wardrobe. He snatched his walkie-talkie and his wooden training sword off his nightstand, sheathed his sword into his belt loop, and escaped out the front door. His father stayed snoozing in his bed.

Ned held the 'ON' button on the walkie-talkie until a small green light flashed from it. He pressed down the button on the side and talked into the speaker on the front.

"Charles, you there? Over." Ned started down the sidewalk, into the Town Square where he would meet his best friend, Charles Addams.

Then, the scratchy-radio voice of a boy came from the walkie-talkie. "Yup, I'm at Mr. Basin's hunting shed. I bought some supplies for the trip, over."

"Okay, stay there I'm coming your way. Over and out." Ned replied in a whisper. He didn't want to be caught, because everyone sort-of knew who he was, but more importantly who his dad was. He pulled his deep red parka hood over his head farther, so the fur lining the hood might hide his face better. He had three layers on, but the sweater that poked from behind his parka was a dark pine-green and knitted in a neat fishtail pattern. His hands were concealed by navy blue gloves, and they were currently being used to hold his supply bag. Ned's blue jeans were tucked into his white snow boots.

Finally, Ned reached his destination. Charles' hands were laced with white silk gloves that extended to his elbows, but his cream-colored button-up blazer's sleeves covered them up to his wrists. Ned believed with all his soul that Charles' favorite color was white, but Charles insisted it was a peachy shade of pink. Under his blazer he wore a snow-white button-up, its collar poking out and folded over the blazer. Of course, Charles' snow-white skinny-fit pants were as fashionable as he could make them. The only color on him was his peachy-pink hair and his brown knee-high boots with small heels on them. His skin was the color of golden oak wood.

"Took you long enough! Did you bring your share of the supplies?" Charles sassed, rolling his eyes.

"Obviously," Ned replied. "I planned this, didn't I?" Ned placed his backpack on the counter of the hunter's shed next to them, at which Mr. Basin never stood unless you rang the bell, because no one on this side of town needed to hunt. "What'd ya get here?"

"I got some snacks, because duh. I also got this pocketknife, just in case. I didn't bring a lot of money." Charles pulled the items out of his satchel, showing them off to Ned.

"Alright, let's go!" Ned asserted, taking a map out of his bag. He gestured for Charles to follow him as he walked out of the town square. Small talk about school, sports, and how they'd befriend a magic spirit ensued for a while until the two boys reached the edge of the Cidairan forest. They stared up at it in awe, in silence. Each tree must have been fifty feet tall. Heaps of snow weighed them down, but their large, sturdy trunks rooted them into the ground.

"Wow," Charles muttered. "It's so... big." He reached into his bag and pulled out an apple, taking a big bite.

"Yeah..." Ned responded. "Let's go." Ned started into the forest, holding onto

His backpack straps. Charles followed along. As they headed off into the woods, the boys began to seem smaller and smaller compared to the enormous pine trees. It seemed to stretch for eternity and they felt they hadn't gained an inch.

"Gosh, haven't we gotten anywhere? I don't think we're gonna find anyone in this, dude." Charles complained, stopping.

"Well, why don't we split up?" Ned offered, turning to his friend.

"Are you kidding? that's how everyone dies in plays!" Charles shouted, waving his arms in the air as if he were signaling a boat.

"Yeah, but we aren't in a play and we aren't looking for something evil." Ned replied, grabbing Charles' arm and dragging him through the forest hastily. Charles quickly pulled away from his grasp, putting his hands on his hips and furrowing his brow.

"I am not going out by myself. This is literally an enchanted forest! We aren't in the T.O.Y. workforce!" Charles stopped, realizing Ned's attention had drifted elsewhere. Of course.

"You hear that?" uttered Ned, looking up and around at the trees. There was rustling in the leaves. Small voices whispered from all directions. Charles flipped open his satchel and pulled out the pocket-knife. Charles popped the blade from its handle and twirled it gracefully in his fingers as if it were a pencil.

As the two stood back-to-back, Ned looked in his backpack for a weapon. Nothing. The only thing he had on him was an old wooden sword.

"Addams, please tell me you have another knife." Ned pleaded, praying that he didn't have just a rotting wood sword for defense. He knew when he needed to hide their identities, and now was that time. Usually, they used last names. This rule applies to everyone except Ned because if his last name was heard by a bad guy, he'd be a target for sure. So, his code name was Comet.

"Negative, Comet. You didn't bring one?" Charles replied hastily. Secretly he loved using terms like those. Charles enjoyed the safety of his friend. Charles could always hide behind Ned from bullies, because those bullies couldn't beat Ned in a fight if they tried. And try they did. But no, Charles is untouchable because his best friend is The Nutcracker's son.

"Just this old wooden sword." Ned felt vines crawl up his feet. Charcoal colored- almost dead. He unsheathed his sword and hacked at them, but to no avail. "Addams!"

Charles was already at his feet. The vines were already rotting so it wasn't hard to get them off. Ned pulled him up and they ran. No matter how small they looked, they were incredibly fast. Thanks to training led by Ned's father and his second in command- Commander Aidan. They were very ready for these scenarios. The whispers got louder- and seemingly closer. He could see gargoyles chasing them out of the corner of his eye. Why were they here? Did they want him, or did they just happen to be here at the wrong time?

Lost in thought, Ned stopped paying attention to where he was going. He tripped over a raised root. Charles stopped to pull him back to his feet, but a gargoyle swept him up by the shoulders with its talons and out of Charles' reach.

"Addams! Go, go, go!" Ned waved him off as he was carried away by the gargoyle. "Go get help!"

Almost Immediately, Ned was so far away that he couldn't see Charles. With his sword still in hand, he bashed at the gargoyle, over and over, until it finally got tired of his antics and dropped him. Throughout all his training, he never trained for falling without a parachute.

Ned hit the ground and was slightly cushioned by the snow. He was cold, and his clothes were wet. Ned looked up and saw a girl that shone like the sun. She didn't seem like anyone else he'd met before- her skin shone soft orange. Her hair contrasted the brightness of her skin with a dark green like the evergreen trees that stood around them. Her hair was long enough to reach her elbows at her side, it swayed in the wind next to the simple green dress she wore. The girl looked to be around his age. Ned looked up at him, and she stared back. Both knew that it was not every day that a boy falls out of the sky.

Ned stood up slowly, noticing the glow of her skin and bright green eyes that seemed to glimmer in the sunlight that poured through the leaves of the trees.

"Uh, hello," Ned attempted, noticing her confused expression. "We need to get out of here, it's dangerous."

"Ah, yes." She spoke, seemingly flustered about the situation around them. "I suppose so, but they would follow me anyhow."

"Why's that?" Ned asked, but before she could answer a small gargoyle landed roughly next to them. She stood up, and pointed at the girl standing next to Ned. That's when Ned started to understand what was happening.

"Ha! I'm gonna be the one to get you, Spirit!" The gargoyle growled as she held her palms out, as if a weapon would appear in her hand. She didn't look much older than either of them- she must have been a trainee like Ned was.

The gargoyle calling the girl a spirit concluded Ned's suspicions- he found the spirit he was looking for. And he wasn't about to let someone kidnap her.

"What, I'm not meeting your kidnap standards?" Ned said, stepping in front of the girl. Ned realized that the spirit could probably protect herself *and* him at the same time, but he was going to try his best anyway. This gargoyle didn't know why Ned should meet her kidnap standards, and he planned to keep it away.

"No, why would I care about some random human." She retorted, rapidly throwing an ornament at them. Reflexively, Ned deflected the ornament upward with his sword. But, out of the corner of his eye, he could see the ornament explode in an entourage of purple and pink flames.

Ned quickly realized he was facing real magic, and real threats.

And he was *not* a real soldier.

The gargoyle came charging at them. Ned prepared himself to fight. Unexpectedly, the gargoyle jumped, with the boost of her gray, stone-like wings she propelled upwards, then forwards. Before Ned could turn, she smashed the ornament into the back of his head. He shot downwards into the snow, face-planting. Ned regained his footing quickly and charged at the gargoyle. He examined her armor- chest, shoulders, elbows, hands, and knees were protected by metal plates. The rest of it was leather belt-like straps to keep the armor secure. She wore brown hunting boots that rose halfway above her shins. Her hair was a deep black- like looking into a cave. She had horns that held the hair out of her face, except for bangs that came through the middle of them. Her hair fell all the way down just past her waist.

Ned noted that her stomach had no armor on it and concluded that would be his target.

So he thrust his sword into her gut, and even though it wasn't sharp enough to cause real damage, she was thrown back and fell into the snow. She pushed herself up and sprinted towards him. But before she could do anything, an orange fireball burned through her wing. However, the spell continued through the wing at Ned's face. He attempted to dodge it, but it sliced his left ear clean off- it fell, bloody cartilage dying the snow.

Injured, the young gargoyle attempted to fly away, but the hole in her wing wouldn't allow it. Instead, she fled the scene.

"I am so sorry, let me help you." The spirit asked worriedly. Ned's head was bleeding profusely. After a blow to the back of the head and loss of an ear, he was overwhelmed with pain. Ned took a knee so that he wouldn't fall over.

"It's okay, you missed my head. Mostly." Ned remarked forgivingly, knowing that it wasn't her intent to hit him. After all, it could've been a lot worse. " Thank you for taking care of the gargoyle. I'm Ned. What's your name?"

"I'm Carol," She replied calmly while tying a handkerchief around his wound. "I'm afraid I have to leave now Ned. I don't want any more of your people injured. It was nice to meet you, though."

Before Ned could muster the energy for a reply, she was gone. He heard Charles' and his father's calls for him, but that was the last thing he remembered of that night.

One

Enlistment Is Like Signing Up For Summer Camp

"Ready?" I asked Charles, as we stood in front of the gates to the biggest military base in the kingdom. It was placed in the capital, where we grew up, so we spent our whole childhood walking past it and seeing it. If we got lucky, my dad would take us in to see it.

"As I'll ever be," Charles replied with a nervous sigh. "We're both gonna be in the same team, right?"

"Duh," I answered, concerned that he even needed to ask that. "There's no one in this crowd smarter than you, Charles."

"What's my brain gonna do when I'm in a standoff with ten gargoyles?"

"Beat them," I answered, refusing to underestimate my best friend's skill.

"Easy to say when you're six-foot-six and have the body of a god." Charles scoffed.

He wasn't wrong- I'd always been conventionally attractive and athletic. Aside from the raging scar on the left side of my head, I was any average person's dreamboat.

""You're agile, Charles. You're slick enough to not get into that standoff. And since you're shorter, you can dodge and weave easily." I assured him.

"Uh- huh," Charles stopped listening.

I shook my head and looked around the crowd. There was an insane amount of people here, probably the most amount of people that had ever joined the military at once before.

Just before I got lost in thought, we were startled by the loud, rustic gates opening on the other end of the courtyard. When I looked up, I saw more than the gates. I saw the Generals Aidan, Codagh, and Crixus-Wells ride through the gates on horseback. They grabbed every-one's attention; they were like the three musketeers.

As the attention moved, I didn't realize that previously, some people's eyes had been on me.

Soon after the generals came through, so did King Klaus. Every-one stared. He didn't ride on horseback- he rode in a golden glittering carriage through the gate. It shone in the mid-day sun blindingly, yet it couldn't take the attention from King Claus, draped in yellow and white, his tucked-in velvety shirt just barely held his gut into his trou-sers, with the help of a thick black belt. His black boots rose to his mid calf, and his snowy white beard fell past his chest, and his hair extended almost that length. Despite his intimidating and powerful appearance, King Claus was kind and gentle. He didn't enjoy parades celebrating only him- which is why he always had the generals approach first.

Then, General Aidan lowered from his horse and walked forward, in an orderly yet frightening fashion. His white uniform seemed to glow on his dark skin- and his narrow black eyes kept steady in front of him- I could hear him arguing with the other Generals behind him about how they came unprepared. Generals Codagh and Crixus tried but failed to keep their snickers in on their horses behind him.

General Aidan's voice boomed: "Soldiers! Forward Face!" And on command, as if second nature, all of us turned and saluted. All our eye-brows furrowed, as if to change from an excited, hopeful expression to that of earnestness and resolve.

"All you Cadets have graduated from your respective universities!"

he continued, equally as loud as before and pacing left to right. "And you all have graduated from boot camp! Yes!?"

"Yes!" everyone shouted in unison.

"All that was practice! Once you go through these doors, you are a soldier!" He shouted, loud enough so that everyone could hear him without a microphone.

"Yes!" everyone shouted again, in unison.

"Now! An introduction statement from your king. Your Commanders will introduce themselves once you have been organized into your branches and your teams." As General Aidan parted with those words, he turned, and marched back to his horse, his medals and awards clanking and jingling the whole way back.

He seemed relieved to go back.

"Thank you, General Aidan, for your informative introduction!" King Klaus said with a chuckle, "You all have worked very hard to get where you are today, and I know you will go far and succeed in your ventures beyond these gates." The King's voice was already loud enough, he didn't have to try at all to be loud, unlike General Aidan. "I am very excited to have you all work in our incredible teams to serve our kingdom. I trust my advisors' judgements on all of you and your rankings and how you will prosper in your positions! Thank you all and let us proceed with this process!" King closed out with a friendly wave and a deep laugh.

And as King Claus' carriage turned, and so did the generals on their horses. The king moved out of the way; and the generals rode off into their three different sections, where the commanders were waiting for them. The rest of us took off behind them to get in.

"So, I guess I'll see you later?" Charles turned to me as he slung his bag over his shoulder and hat, which he somehow managed to tuck all his hair into. The big, fluffy mess was a struggle to hide- he had considered cutting short but decided against it. Charles almost looked like a different person with his hair pulled back and wearing his dark red Cadet uniform.

"Yeah," I said, with a sigh. I felt nervous and almost sick. I knew I had nothing to fear, but now that I'm doing it, becoming a soldier seems more serious than it did five months ago at boot camp. "Remember, we need to get people for our team,"

He nodded in agreement and then we headed our separate ways. As I walked down the center pathway, I could feel eyes on me. It felt like they were burning through me- not cold, but curious. It hadn't been the first time that someone wanted to 'be friends' with me because of my family status. As I got closer to the front of the line, I got more looks from more people. Then the commanders looked.

Then General Aidan looked.

Then I got to the front of the line. Commander Packer looked at me with a sort of smug grin, then asked, "What's your last name, kid?"

All the commanders call us Cadets "Kid" because to them, we probably look like toddlers. But what confused me the most was why he even asked my name- I responded anyway- "Nutcracker,"

Not a split second later, Commander Packer was laughing so hard he held his stomach, then he held out his hand. Commander Manning slapped his hand to his face and sighed disappointedly as he handed him a twenty-dollar bill.

And I could do nothing but stand there.

"Yeah, I told you it was him! He looks just like General Navid!"

"Whatever, the kid has white hair at the age of twenty-three and his dad is just starting to get gray now!" Commander Manning argued.

"You two need to get your act together," rebutted Commander Woodlaine, "Sorry about these two, Nedrall, They're like this during training hours too."

I started to respond but couldn't finish.

"Ah, C'mon Auden, it's just a little bet. Anyways- Cadet Nedrall, you're in the first subpartment, now get outta here." She explained playfully but in a hurried manner, a lot of people were behind me, so it was understandable why. It was also a relief to not be asked questions once my name had been pronounced. Although as I started to head over to my subpartment, some of the other Cadets looked at me, all with different expressions. When I got to my group, some of them slouched.

But as I put my bags on the floor, I looked upon 99 Cadets of subpartment 1, and most of them were celebrating amongst each other- it felt selfish to think they cheered for me, but in all honesty, it was probably true.

Two Cadets, one large and the other small, stepped towards me happily. Getting a better look at them, I saw that the girl, who was abnormally tall, and was astonishingly symmetrical. Not one thing was unlike the other on either side. Her skin was a warm sepia color, but down the middle of her face was a symmetric pattern of vitiligo. It danced down her forehead onto the bridge of her nose, and finally across her lips to her chin, where it stopped. The vitiligo reached the inner corners of her eyes and the edge of her eyebrows, collecting the pigment from her skin. Even her hair was braided tightly and neatly into two twin braids. And if I thought I towered over people before, she was a skyscraper. The girl was almost a head and a half taller than me.

The other one, however, looked much simpler. His hair was loosely curly and just long enough to cover his ears and was an orangey-blonde. He was a bit shorter than me, but he sure was built. The guy looked like he could lift carriages with one arm. His green eyes contrasted his yellowish terracotta skin tones, and brought forth the dark freckles that poked his face all over.

"Hey! You're General Nutcracker's son aren't you? Dude! How cool is that?!" He seemed over-excited, like I lived in some glorious palace like the king. "I'm Dante, and this is Fayola." Fayola waved to me with a welcoming smile.

"It's nice to meet you, I'm Nedrall, but you can just call me Ned." I tried to avoid the topic of my dad in introductory conversation, it felt self-centered.

"Cool," he remarked casually, "They're just about done with enlistment, we should probably head over to the stairs with everyone else." The two turned around and ushered me to the stairs into the base, where General Aidan and the rest of the commanders stood atop the stairs. People crowded closer together near the stage and I could feel the heat of 99 of my peers and the humid air of late summer, trapped in this military base entrance. My back hurt from carrying all my stuff, but I figured we'd get to our quarters soon enough. I was wrong.

General Aidan started to speak.

"We've changed how we're quartering you all, men and women will be in separate rooms, but not in separate buildings. If there is any funny business-" He cut himself off for a moment, and seemed disappointed or embarrassed that he just said, "Funny business,". He continued, "You will be cut and will not have any second chances. Do I make myself clear?"

"Yes!" All our voices boomed in sync. If our voices were anything less than perfect, we'd all owe General Aidan laps around the entire perimeter of the base.

Two

We'll Let Them Beat Each Other Up To Prove How Well They Work Together

We were all released a few at a time, starting with my team, thankfully. In all the rush, I almost got lost from Dante and Fayola. I looked carefully at each sign above the rooms once I reached the inside of the building.

"Well, if it isn't Mr. Nedrall! I guess you know your way around already." Dante announced, jogging towards me, trying not to get in anyone's way.

"Hey Dante, where is your quarter?" I replied, forcing a friendly tone over an awkward one.

"I'm in G22, how about you? Are we close? Because if we roomed together that would be crazy." He seemed eager to be my friend, but I think that was just because of his personality, not mine.

"Wow! We are! That's crazy!" I said, genuinely shocked at the chances of this happening. Fate works in mysterious ways, usually not as obvious as this, but I'll take it.

"Nice! Lead the way, Nutcracker! Also, have you seen Fayola around? I'm trying to spot her, but I can't see over these people."

Without responding, I looked up away from him and searched for her. She should be easy to spot, with her hair and height. After a few moments, I saw a head above the crowd with black braids.

"I see her! Follow me." I glanced towards Dante and ushered him to follow but kept focus on Fayola, so I didn't lose her. We shuffled through the slowly dying crowd to where she was- she wasn't moving fast and kept changing direction. She was probably lost, and Dante was probably going to leave our quartering area to help Fayola find hers.

We caught up, and I called out to her: "Hey! Fayola!" She stopped to turn, looking relieved to see a familiar face. She smiled back, flustered.

"Hey! You having trouble finding your room?" Dante questioned. She nodded and signed to us 'F98 is my room, can you help me?'.

"Sure," I replied. I wanted to be friendly to her and Dante, I had a good feeling about them. "Me and Dante are roomed together in G22, we shouldn't be too far from each other." We went back to where we came from but turned left to go to the F wing. A few minutes later, we were at F98. "Here we are! See ya at the arena tomorrow!" Dante exclaimed, giving Fayola back her bag that he carried for her. I don't doubt that it wouldn't have been a struggle for Fayola to carry it herself, but I guess she knew that he enjoyed helping people. She signed, 'I will see you tomorrow, good night!'

"What? Good night? But it's only-" As I said this, I looked at my watch, and the time seemed to halt my words. "How is it 11:30 already? We have half an hour until curfew!" I blurted, baffled by how the time flew.

"Geez, it really is late, huh?" Dante sighed. "Well, we should get back- meet our other roommates and unpack."

We started walking towards our room side by side. Background noise of other people looking for their rooms filled the silence for a while.

"Is it weird to ask what it's like to be the Nutcracker's son?" Dante asked.

"Eh, not really. I'm used to it. A lot of people think it's some grand luxury but it's really not." I answered casually.

"I figured you and your dad lived in some mansion. Fay and I grew up as neighbors out in the country. My family runs a farm and Fay's family hunts. She's the best hunter out there, the town jewel. She's the oldest of like, eleven siblings. I just help around the farm and whatnot, we both figured life would be more exciting and fulfilling here." Dante explained.

"No, we don't have a mansion. We could, I guess, but we don't. I grew up here in the capital with Charles. But it's good that you and Fayola have that one up on me. You guys know how to survive in the wild, meanwhile I went out to the woods one time as a kid and I lost my ear." I answered, turning my scar towards Dante, so that he could see it.

"Dude! That's a sick scar, what even happened!?" Dante gasped, covering his mouth with his hand.

"It's hard to remember, to be honest." I lied. Nobody besides Charles and my dad believed me when I told them what happened.

"Ouch. Must've got a mad concussion from that."

"Oh for sure. I couldn't hear anything for weeks, much less train. And then, y'know, there's the whole being half-deaf thing." I replied, remembering how often I'd have to yell 'What?' at people just to get them to repeat themselves more loudly.

"You must've done some crazy shit as a kid if you've landed as the highest-ranking Cadet in the workforce without an ear." Dante laughed.

"Yup. If there were two words to describe my life thus far it would be training and crazy shit." I laughed with him. "My friend Charles and I were always up to no good."

"Can't imagine it's easy to get away with stuff when your dad is literally a General of the workforce."

"No, it definitely wasn't, but Charles was always the sneaky one helping me flesh out my outlandish adventures." I agreed. Just then, we found our room- G22.

The door was unlocked, and we walked into a moderately large room, containing two bunk beds, a cot, a nightstand next to the cot, and two desks. It looked like a cheap hotel and smelled like peppermint and fabric cleaner. Three other guys were in there. The first one was about as tall as me and had chestnut colored hair and cold blue eyes. The other two looked identical. They both had black hair and hazel brown eyes. I thought they must be twins. One of the look-alikes started to talk and they both beamed.

"No way! We're rooming with the destiny kid! What's up man, I'm Asam, this is my brother, Basil. It's nice to meet you." Asam stood up to shake my hand.

I shook it firmly but friendly and replied, "The pleasure is all mine," I laughed awkwardly, "That's a nickname I've never heard before, do people call me that?"

"For sure, once word got out that Navid Nutcracker's son got applied for boot camp, you became the destiny kid." Interrupted Basil, who came to Asam's side and held out his own hand.

"Why's that?" I asked.

"Well, y'know," Basil stammered. "You joined the military, like your dad, so it's kinda your destiny."

"Oh, that makes sense," I replied, feeling my nerves spike. *Great, I have a destiny now.* I thought to myself.

"And what's your name?" Asam changed the subject, looking at Dante.

"I'm Dante, it's nice to meetcha," Dante shook his hand excitedly, then Basil. He looked around the room, examining it. "So, I guess the top bunk was first come first serve?" Dante joked.

"Haha, I guess so," Asam laughed. "You two can decide between the bottom bunk or the cot."

"Dibs on the cot!" Dante called. He had a small running start before jumping onto the cot, and landing on it with a bounce and a loud creak.

"Alrighty." I responded. I looked towards the other guy, who was sitting at one of the desks, who was writing like he had a speech tomorrow.

I decided now wasn't the time to make small talk.

With a sigh, I plopped my things on the floor next to my bed. I sat on it, and it creaked. Not nearly as loud as the cot, but squeaky nonetheless. Laying down, I saw the lights go out in the hallway. Must be curfew.

The night grew longer and Dante's snores grew louder. I didn't even notice that the guy that was writing went up to his bed until he sat on it, and I heard the muffled sounds of a squeaky bed. My ear was to the pillow, so I almost missed him talking to me.

"Why'd you come here? Your dad?" He asked the second question with more sympathy than the first.

I didn't even know this guy. But, I guess this is how you get to know people.

"Kinda. I just always wanted to be like him growing up so he helped me get here." I answered.

"I bet he did. My pops told me I needed to come here, I didn't really get a choice." He replied.

"Oh, why?" I asked back. I started to understand what prompted his original question.

"Said I needed to be more of a man. Dunno why, cuz I'm more of a man than *he* is."

"Is he who you were writing to?"

"Yeah. It's funny I roomed with you, he always compared me to you. Growing up here, everyone knew who you were, that you were training with the military, you're learning from the best of the best, yada yada yada." He told me.

I didn't really know how to respond to that. I am a lot of things, but I am not a therapist. I just answered with: "Yeah. Coincidence."

"Just don't show me up," He said, supposedly trying to end the conversation on a macho note.

I rolled my eyes. "I'll try my best."

That morning, bells rang in the hallway. Their ear-piercing ring woke most of us up immediately, but Dante was already up and ready. I didn't expect that from him, he seemed like the type to be a heavy sleeper and wouldn't wake up if a plane crashed in his front yard.

It was 5'oclock in the morning. There were two showers in our restroom, and the twins called dibs first. I didn't plan to take a shower that morning but rather that afternoon, as I had taken a shower yesterday morning. Out of curiosity, I looked up to see what the other guy was doing. I felt like I should say hi, but I wasn't good at that. I didn't really want to talk to him, either. He was sitting upright, stretching his arms and back, he was facing away from me. I decided just to go ahead and put on my uniform. I pulled my second uniform out of my bag and proceeded with the long process of putting on the whole get-up.

I started with the undershirt and pants. The shirt looked like a button up dress shirt, but it had golden braiding down the middle. Despite its looks, it was comfortable to wear when fighting and quite efficient too. Then came the pants. The pants of our uniform were simple but effective. They were stretchable and comfortable, and they didn't look bad, they were a deep iridescent red color. Third was the coat. The coat was generally for show, you didn't wear it on the field. It was red, like the pants, but velvety instead of shiny. We wore them most of the time to show what rank you were and what achievements you had. I then put on my sash, which was golden and silk- and plain. It had no medals on it yet, no rewards for anything. Hopefully I'll change that soon. I strapped on my belt, which had a sheath for two swords. Finally I slipped on my black boots, which came up to just below my knees. They were strapped with buckles and sheaths for things like daggers, knives, and other things in case you were stripped of your sword.

Just then, Asam and Basil slipped out of the restroom wearing their uniforms, with their coats and empty sashes donned. Before Dante and the other guy, whose name I still didn't know, could discuss who went first I hopped up and got to the sink before anyone could object.

"I see how it is, Ned!" Dante called out jokingly as I finished getting ready.

Soon enough, we all were ready and were heading down to the mess hall. I hoped to find Charles and Fayola there so we could build our team before we made official teams. My dad told me that the first mess hall always looked like a series of interviews between the Cadets.

Dante went ahead to look for Fayola, While I got distracted looking at the paintings on the walls. There were paintings of all of the Generals and Commanders. And King Klaus of course. The first painting was of General Crixus-Wells. He had spiky silver hair, sticking up and showing his forehead. He had a diamond shaped face, with the brightest green eyes you could think of. Brighter than Dante's, even. He had more freckles on his face than stars in the galaxy, and teeth whiter than snow. All of the Generals wore the same uniform- just like ours except theirs were white instead of crimson. And their sashes were full and glistening.

I skipped over General Codagh and the rest of their commanders to the General of my division, General Aidan. I looked at him, and it was like he stared right back. His sash was almost blinding with shiny metallic paint, and the reflection of light on his deep black eyes just as bright. His skin was as smooth as pure water, his hair as neat and clean as a new set of knives. He had eyebrows sharper than his glare. There wasn't a hair out of line.

Then were his Commanders: Packer, Manning, and Woodlaine. Their uniforms were again, slightly different. Their suits were deep green like the trees in the Cidarian forest, with brass braids instead of gold like the rest of us. All their sashes were filled up too, it was hard to notice that their sashes were white instead of gold. Commander Packer was muscular. His picture had a wide, genuine grin. He was playful, a joker, and loved making bets with people. And when he lost those bets, he stuck to his word like glue. He had ginger hair that was cut close to his head and had blue eyes as bright as an iced-over lake. His eyebrows were thick but well kept- He had a scar that ran through his right eyebrow across his nose and under his left eye. I don't know where it came from, but it looked like the wound must have been nasty.

Next to Packer was Woodlaine. Commander Woodlaine wasn't the first non-binary person to become a commander, but they were the only one in command at the moment. Commander Woodlaine had a circular face shape and had short, spirally light blonde hair. Their eyes were hazel, a mix of blue and green. They had a few small but noticeable scars- two on their chin, and one on their cheekbone. Their sash was just as shiny as the others, but there was a badge I'd never seen before. It was a circle, no ribbons, but it had stripes- yellow, white, purple and black.

Next was Commander Manning. He had a round face too, and a dark brown beard. Brown beard, brown eyes, brown hair, it must have been either his favorite or least favorite color. His smile shined brighter than his sash, though. He hadn't been commander for as long as the others had.

As I started to head to the mess hall to catch up with Dante and Fayola, I saw a recognizable face walking my way.

"Ned! Hey!" It was Charles. He approached me with a face of relief.

"Charles!" It was great to see him again, the places I'd been were familiar but the people weren't. It was good to see a familiar face.

"What are you doing zoning out in the halls? You're gonna be late!"

"Oh crap," I had forgotten entirely about the arena combats today. Without breakfast in my stomach, I probably wouldn't make it in the run to the arena.

"We should go then," I agreed as we took off running. When we got there, everyone was just about done eating and were starting to leave.

"Uh," Charles looked around, thinking. "Okay, I have snacks on me but I don't know if it'll be enough."

"It's gonna have to do." I replied hastily. Charles presented an apple. Not my favorite options, but it would have to do. I hesitated grabbing the apple.

"Just eat the apple, Ned."

I grabbed it and rolled my eyes.

"Are you going to the arena?" I asked.

"Yeah. I'm in one of the rounds, actually. Dunno who I'm upp against, though, so pray for me I guess."

"Good luck." I replied. I knew Charles wasn't very confident in his combat skills, even if everyone else was. "You've got this."

"Thanks." He said back to me as we parted ways.

I darted toward the fields as I chewed resentfully on the apple Charles gave me. The mess hall was already empty. Eventually, I caught up to the back of the crowd, but couldn't spot Fayola or Dante. When I heard General Aidan's voice, I started listening.

"-Organized sparring. First you will be without weapons, then we will move to weaponry. You will choose from swords, spears, bows, scythes, and many more. If you are first to go, get to the prep area of the arena. If not, get to the stands." General Aidan finished. I couldn't see him, but he was ahead of us, probably with the commanders. I followed everyone else to the stadium. I looked around again for Fayola and spotted her in the front of the group- I also spotted General Aidan, on horseback, and yelling at everyone to catch up. We started running, and I tried to get up to where Fayola was, but it was hard to get around people. After a lot of unnecessary sprinting, we got to the arena and I shifted through the crowd to find Fayola, but without Dante.

"Where's Dante?" I asked, out of breath. Fayola looked unfazed by the run. Catching a horse must be easy when you're right behind it. Fayola pointed down towards the arena circle, and there he was. It made sense for him to be picked for the first fist fight. He was short, but he was pretty built. I knew his punches had to hurt. I looked to the other side of the circle and-

Oh my God.

Of course Dante was fighting the mystery guy, and of course we were all roomed together, and of course this would probably cause problems, and of course this guy looked like the only person in the entire military that was stronger than Dante. The guy was taller than I was, and looked like he was chiseled from diamonds.

Or maybe he wasn't that strong and just looked like he could pinch someone's skull off their shoulders, but had no tactics to do so.

"Hurry up and sit down, we don't have all day," Boomed General Aidan through a loudspeaker. "First up is Dante Garcia and Tyler Brown. You have all done this before; you know the rules. No fatal harm, no broken bones. If they surrender, collapse, or are pinned with their shoulders and knees on the ground for five seconds, that's a loss for them. These are one round fights, so don't embarrass yourself."

And with that, a buzzer blared over everyone's voices and drew their attention to the fighters. They hesitantly approached each other, and Fayola watched intently.

After few seconds of hesitant approach, Tyler charged at Dante, eyes locked on his target. Dante Immediately changed his stance. It changed from a careful approach to a sturdy defense, his arms protecting his head, legs protecting his balance.

Tyler used the momentum from his sprint to undercut Dante's ribcage. He looked winded, but he still stood his ground. Dante grabbed Tyler by his shoulders and knocked him off his feet. Dante backed up as Tyler bounced back to his feet. He charged again. Dante was ready this time- as Tyler went for a right-hand swing, Dante reached across using his right arm and grabbed Tyler's fist. Dante pulled Tyler's fist across his own body and Tyler spun off balance and before he could stand evenly, Dante had tackled him to the ground. Tyler was pinned. No matter how hard he struggled or squirmed, Dante was like a rock on him.

I counted silently. I was rooting for Dante. "One, Two, Three, Four, Five!" I had to shout for the last second, I couldn't keep the excitement in. A buzzer went off and Dante let go. Fayola jumped up beside me, clapping and smiling. People cheered, I cheered, and loudly too.

"Alright!" Aidan shouted on the loudspeaker. "Garcia and Brown, get to the stands. Next up is Paris Fabron and Mack Kingsman."

As everyone settled back down to watch the next fight, Fayola and I searched for Dante in the stands. Fayola spotted him first and waved excitedly. He weaved his way through the lines of people to get to us. On the way here, he got high fives, pats on the back, and cheers. He was eating up the attention.

"So how much did that punch hurt?" I asked, seeing that he was still slightly hunched over and catching his breath.

"Like hell. The guy is three heads taller than me!" he said as Fayola rubbed his head with a grin, messing up his hair on purpose.

As he fixed his hair again, he shot a playful glare at Fayola, and changed his stance proudly. "But I won, so Tyler can suck it!" He and Fayola high-fived.

"You know him?" I asked, curious if he already knew his name before the fight or if he learned it from Aidan's announcement.

"Yeah, we know him." Dante and Fayola shared a knowing look. "He's always been a jerk, takes after his dad on that one. If jealousy was a person, it would be him."

Fayola signed to me: 'He is unnecessarily rude and aggressive, but his home is hurtful to him.'

"Yeah, and he's particularly jealous of you." Dante pointed at me.

"Yeah, I think I understood that much when he decided to finally talk last night after everyone went to sleep," I added.

"What did he say to you?" Dante asked defensively. It was easy to see that he had a specific disdain for Tyler.

"He basically just told me how his dad is a dick and made him join the military so he would be more like me. He told me his dad compares him to me a lot." I explained.

"Well that's not your problem," Dante replied.

Fayola agreed, signing that I should just ignore him and focus on myself.

We continued talking with each other until a buzzer cut us off. I turned to see a petite blonde girl pinned into the dirt by a burly bearded man. She looked bloodied up. I hadn't paid attention to the fight, but when I focused in everyone started booing the winner. Through the berating and chewing out, the girl was escorted out of the arena by Commander Woodlaine, who seemed like they were tending to the girl's wounds as she walked, and the girl's opponent was getting aggressively reprimanded by Commander Packer.

"Next up, Charles Addams and Fayola Abiodun." Aidan announced.

I just stood there, shocked. How does this stuff happen? Dante and Fayola were pumped, though.

"You got this!" I told her as she walked off, I don't know if I meant it or not. I'd never seen her in action, but I grew up with Charles. He was agile and quick.

"Fay prefers a weapon to fist-fighting, but I'm sure she can handle this. Don't you know this other guy? Is he any good?" Dante asked.

"Charles is better with a weapon too, but people always tend to underestimate him. He's smart; he can read his opponent unlike any other, and people mistake his size for weakness. He's agile and quick."

"Then I think he and Fayola will be a good match." Dante didn't tell me much about Fayola's strengths, but I was about to find out.

As they entered the arena, I could feel the uncertainty that the two of them felt. I could see the gears in their heads turning. Charles approached her carefully, examining her. Fayola did the same, but seemed less cautious. I could tell by her face what she was thinking. She wanted to pin him down and be done with it. He wasn't that easy. Fayola hastily sprinted at him, plowing through the air like a jet. I think if Fayola sprinted at me like that I'd pass out on the spot.

Charles started at her as well, matching her speed. Fayola lowered stance to a tackling position, but Charles dropped further. Just as they were about to collide, Charles pushed off the ground to the left- he landed in a sideways lunge and as Fayola started to trip over his leg, she reached out to push him over, her long arms stretching like wings. they tumbled, and Charles was on his back. He reflexively rolled to his side. He swiftly brought his legs under him. Before he could stand, Fayola was on top of him. She knocked him off of his knees and pinned him into the dirt.

"One.. Two.." I counted in sync with Aidan. I wanted Charles to win. I knew he could. "...Three.. Fo-" And then, just before Aidan could count to four, Charles did something.

He grabbed her shoulders and pushed them up, so that his arms would extend and remove his shoulders from the ground. He brought up his legs and kicked her just above her waist. She toppled over him and Charles quickly but carefully rose to his feet. Without wasting time, Charles leapt at her, and pushed her shoulders down- but Fayola had other plans.

Fayola and Charles struggled to get one another down. Tussling, tugging at sleeves and slamming shoulders into the dust. Finally, Charles got Fayola on her back, her right arm underneath her and Charles' leg holding down the other arm. His hands gripped her shoulders, but he was careful not to put a harmful amount of pressure on her arms- he didn't want to break any bones.

"One.. Two.. Three.. Four.." Aidan counted.

"Five!" I exclaimed, jumping to my feet and punching the air to exert my ecstatic energy. I cheered enthusiastically as Charles bounced up, and reached down to help Fayola.

"Wow," Dante stammered. "That was a great fight! Fay just about did it! But Charles- man that guy is quick. I think it was the size difference that made it the most interesting, what do you think?"

I never noticed how much Dante analyzed people's skills. He was incredible at reading people. "I think you're right," I finally responded. "Fayola being as tall as she is, compared to Charles, the only reason he really won is because he's so much smaller than her. But on the other hand, the only reason she could pin him down was because she is a lot bigger than him."

"Exactly! C'mon, let's go find them." As we left, Aidan was announcing the next two people to fight. The last round of fist fighting was starting, then we'd move to weaponry. I had a feeling they were going to want to see if I'm as good as dad boasts about, but that might be the pride in me talking. We got out of the stands and made our way to the end of the hallway. I saw Charles walking down the hallway, looking as carefree as ever. He was wrapping his knuckles and wrists with bandages and his chin had scratch marks on them, probably a result of Fayola struggling to get back up.

"Hey Ned!" Charles smiled and waved to me, and as he approached us, he held out his wrapped hand to Dante. "I'm Charles, Ned probably told you that, but it's great to meet you."

"He did, my name's Dante, the way you fought out there was incredible! I was stunned!" Dante blurted out. He seemed to be almost entranced by Charles' performance in the arena.

"Thanks, it was really difficult. She's really good, but she didn't say anything when I helped her up. She smiled at me, but didn't talk. So I didn't talk either. It was awkward, honestly." Charles scratched the back of his neck, avoiding eye contact and looking down at our shoes.

"Yeah, Fayola's mute, she does sign language though." I answered, putting my hands in my pockets and looking back down the hallway that Dante and I came from. "Let's get going, see if we can find her." They nodded and we started down the corridor.

"So, I overheard the Commanders and Aidan talking." Charles started, still looking at the floor. "Our first mission is starting sooner rather than later. The word going around is that the gargoyles have been planning an ambush near the capitol. The generals say it'll be in the Cidarian forest."

"Geez, the gargoyles can't stay outta there huh?" Dante asked. I remembered fighting a gargoyle with a wooden sword, and I remembered seeing the Christmas Spirit. Everyone told me that it was my memories messing with me, but Dad and Charles believed me. Dad told me that she shows up to special people, who are meant to do great things. I think that was just to make me feel better about the situation. That was the night I lost my ear, and it was kind of a mess. I wondered if she would be in the forest again, maybe she'd help me like she did when I was ten.

I decided not to hide this event from Dante, especially considering Chalres is here now. "Yup, I actually was in the forest the first time they attacked; it was crazy." That was the only way I could describe it. Crazy.

"*We* were." Charles corrected. "Because Ned wanted to find The Christmas Spirit."

"Seriously? What a terrible coincidence. The day you go ghost hunting is the day that the gargoyles attack. Did you find her at least? The Christmas Spirit?" Dante asked.

"I did. Charles and I got separated and I had to fight a gargoyle. She wanted The Christmas Spirit for some reason, and she didn't look a lot older than me at the time, honestly. If it had been an adult I probably would've died."

"Geez-" Dante started, but was interrupted by Charles.

"And they say they're drafting physically able veterans for this ambush because they think it'll be that bad." Charles nervously stated in what seemed like one breath. When he finished talking, he held his breath and waited for a reaction. He looked at me.

"Oh." was all I could muster out. Dante didn't speak, he probably felt the same weight I did. My dad is a physically able veteran. My chest felt like lead, sinking into the bottom of my stomach. Honestly, I should have known better than to feel this nervous, I've felt this way a million times before.

The feeling disappeared when I saw Fayola in the stands waving at us. We talked for a while, until all of the sparring was over. By that point, the sun was almost below the horizon, but could still light our way back to the base. Aidan told us on the way back that we would all be briefed over our radios about what course of action we would take before the ambush. There were still a lot of things to prepare for.

Three

Is It Too Late To Use The Bathroom?

There was still some time left before we had to be with our teams-but mine still wasn't complete. Like the adults we are, we were allowed to pick our teams ourselves. With Charles, Dante, Fayola, and myself, we needed one more person to make a team of five. As we thought about our options, we realized we needed someone from E.L.F. branch.

That's when I felt a tap on my shoulder. I looked behind me, then I had to look down to see her face. She was seriously small, and I started to wonder how she graduated from boot camp, but I told myself to not underestimate her.

"Uhm, so, do you guys have an open spot on your team? I know I'm not anywhere close to intimidating but I'm fast and good with a bow and-" She started to ramble. Then I recognized her as the girl that got pummeled by some big burly Cadet on the first day of sparring.

"Are you an E.L.F.?" I cut her off mid-sentence, but she didn't seem bothered.

"Uh, yes."

"Yeah! We actually needed one on our team. There's a spot left." I assured her and looked back to the rest of my team for approval. All of them agreed, but Fayola seemed particularly excited. She walked over and smiled down at her. If Fayola towered over Charles, she was a skyscraper compared to this girl. Fayola signed to her: "Finally a woman! What is your name?"

"Paris!" She responded. "Thank you so much, nobody else wanted me on their team after I embarrassed myself a week ago."

Looking down at her, I noticed her eyes were unnaturally light. They were a baby blue color, like ocean waves in the morning. Her hair was just as light, she had sandy-blonde twin buns, and bangs that stretched just below her neatly kept eyebrows.

"Welcome to the team, Paris!" Dante greeted. "And you didn't embarrass yourself, that guy was just an-"

"A what?" said a deep, rough voice. I turned to see who was trying to cause trouble, and it was Mack. The guy that had to get buzzed out because of the excessive force in the arena. His team was behind him, like some gang of high school bullies.

"We're stationed near each other. watch how you talk," he threatened.

Now, I don't like to play the mean card, but this guy deserved it.

"Stay in your lane, Mack." I glared at him, and his eyes looked like they wanted to say something, but his mouth knew he shouldn't.

Tyler stepped forward. "I hope you don't think that just because your daddy's here he's gonna protect you."

"I don't need him to protect me. If anything, he needs to protect you *from* me." I snapped, and he knew I was right. I didn't want to waste any more time with them, so I turned back to my team. Dante and Fayola looked stunned but proud. Charles' face seemed to say 'Yeah, that's right. Don't mess with him.'

Paris didn't dare raise her gaze from the floor.

"Let's get to our stations. We're done here. Is everyone ready?" I asked, looking to make sure they all had their stuff.

"Yeah, we're ready." Dante answered. The tension dropped as everyone prepared to start our first mission.

"What does that guy have against you, anyway?" Paris asked me as we started walking away.

"He doesn't like me because his dad is an asshole and not famous, unlike my dad." I answered when we got outside. Seeing the treeline in the distance, the reality of being in a battle started to crawl under my skin.

"Ugh. Annoying." Paris rolled her eyes.

Charles butted into the conversation. "Oh yeah, all the shit he gets for just existing? You'd be surprised how many people are jealous of him."

"Hell, It's not that surprising how many people are jealous of him." Dante followed. "It's the people that are jerks about it that are the problem."

"Yeah, true." Paris agreed.

I wasn't sure how comfortable I was talking about people being jealous of me- to be honest it was hard to see what people could be jealous of in me.

When we snuck outside to the woods, the air was sharp and bitterly cold. all of our noses and cheeks turned pink as we trudged through the snow. Eventually, we reached the treeline and crouched, waiting.

Each of us were crouched behind a tree, observing our surroundings. We knew the gargoyles could attack from any direction- from the sky or on foot, even through manipulating dead roots they could pull us into the dirt. Everyone's hand lay waiting on their weapon as snow fell silently through the air.

It felt like an hour had passed before anything happened. I saw something gray rip through the air. Then another. And another. They shot down at us, arrows coming down like lightning one at a time. Fayola shot down two gargoyles with her bow, and I impaled one with my sword as they flew down. I heard one land behind me. Before he could stab me with his dagger, I turned. I used the other gargoyle, still impaled by my sword, to shield me. I let the gargoyle slide off my sword as the other one unsheathed his own. I knew I had to attack it with full force, since gargoyle's skin is much thicker and tougher than my own. I swung upwards at it and he jumped back to dodge.I took this opportunity to charge at it, and swung downwards. My sword slashed cleanly across his chest. I backed up in case he wasn't finished yet. He dashed towards me, his sword sticking straight ahead of him. There was too little reaction time to move my feet. I spun to the side, his sword missing me by mere centimeters. With the momentum of my spin, I stabbed him in his back. Pulling my sword out of his back, I looked around hastily to find my team. They were all still there. Fayola was fighting with Paris and Charles and Dante were a few yards away from me on the sides.

"Are y'all okay?" Charles asked breathlessly. We all breathed heavily, processing our first real encounters with gargoyles.

Well, first for all of them.

"Yeah," Dante answered.

"We're okay." Paris replied, and Fayola nodded.

"I'm good, let's move up" I waved my hand as a motion to start following me. We started running into the forest. Our breaths were like train steam, rising up then falling behind us as we pushed through the snow. As I led, Paris kept up with me. I could tell she was going slower to match my pace.

"Paris, lead the way. I'll stay at the caboose." I slowed for a moment until I was in the back of the group.

"Uh, okay," Paris responded with a light breath. "Keep going this way." We were slowed down by constant run-ins with Gargoyle troops, and luckily we weren't injured.

We came to a stop.

"This should be where the next team is- where are they?" Paris stuttered, fiddling with her sword handle and darting her eyes around. I looked up, the sky was shielded by trees. It was too silent.

Then, out of the snowy branches, a gargoyle troop attacked us. We were surrounded. Fayola shot an arrow at one, and Dante held his spear ready. They were on us in a heartbeat. They clawed, we swung, then they backed off for a moment. But only for a moment. One of them grabbed Fayola by her biceps using his talons. As she struggled, Dante instantly started ripping and tugging at the enemy's talons. I wanted to help, I really did, but the other gargoyles kept me too busy to do anything else. Charles had the same sorry expression as I did.

Dante's struggles were to no avail, and the gargoyle flew off with Fayola in his claws. I used Paris' bow to try to shoot him down. It missed. I stood still, the bow still aimed at the sky. There were no arrows left. Dante's yell echoed throughout the forest, every time it came back it was filled with the same pain as the first one. Paris gasped and tears ran down her pink cheeks.

I couldn't say anything at all.

"NED!" Charles screamed out after he came to his senses, after what we witnessed. Before I knew it, a gargoyle latched onto my shoulders. He started to fly off, but Dante grabbed my legs. He struggled to keep his feet on the ground and I tried to loosen the gargoyle's grip. Dante slipped on the icy ground, falling onto his back. In a panic, I grabbed a tree branch. Charles grabbed my hand, and Dante grabbed Charles' other hand as they desperately tried to match the strength of the gargoyle's enourmous wings. I knew what would happen if I let go, if Charles slipped. The gargoyle would fly away with all of us and drop us from way above the trees. I was a lot bigger than I was when I was a kid. Snow wouldn't break my fall this time. I looked around me, no gargoyles. I looked at Charles. He looked desperate. I knew if I kept struggling, and if we won, we'd all be on the ground, with a gargoyle above us.

I could only think of one solution that resulted in as little casualties and injuries as possible.

I let go. In an instant, I was brought above the trees, fighting, grabbing at the gargoyle's wings. As I was taken away, I could hear Charles. I couldn't tell what he was saying, but I hoped that another one wouldn't come for them. In an opening of the branches, I saw a glimpse of Paris sprinting away. I took my sword and flung it around above me, hoping that I'd hit something.

I did, and I fell. I fell into what seemed like the hotspot of the ambush. I was falling too fast to grab a branch. I was falling too fast to think. I shut my eyes and-

-and I landed. On something. I opened my eyes and I was in a net. I could see something charging at me, and I shut my eyes again. Then I fell again, sensing the familiar feeling of landing in snow.

"Nutcracker! Why are you here, and where's your team?!" General Aidan demanded.

"I- a gargoyle grabbed and flew away with me and the same happened to Fayola. The rest of them are still there, sir." I quickly rose to my feet.

"Kid, the sweet spot is their achilles. Cut the achilles."

"Yes Sir." That would've been great to know.

"Get back to your group, and fast. Find Cadets Fayola with your team and then stop wasting time."

"Yes sir." I turned and ran off in the direction I thought I should be going. I started running along a river. While running, I wondered why my dad wasn't with General Aidan. He was in the team as General Aidan, so why weren't they together when Aidan cut me loose? I ran down the river, and saw a gargoyle perched on a fallen tree. She looked familiar to me, although I didn't know why. She turned to me, but as I ran at her, she grinned. She didn't attack me, or even defend herself. She just grinned and flew away. I brushed it off, starting to cross back over the river that the gargoyle carried me over. I plowed my feet through the shallow water, trying not to let it push my feet out from underneath me. The water was cold but I pushed through. My tall boots kept the water away from my feet. I tried to dry my boots when I got to the other side so the snow wouldn't stick to them.

I shook it off. The cold wasn't anything new, and it doesn't bother me anyway.

I looked around, trying to assess where I was. This was a huge forest, so the landmarks were hard to memorize. After seeing the edge of Sanjor Cliff, I realized I was at Wespon Run river. Just when I started to feel comfortable in my situation, my heart was ripped out of my chest. I heard an all too familiar voice. It wasn't in strength, or pride, or victory. It howled in pain.

I sprinted towards it. There was no way this was real. I was dreaming.

I was in a nightmare.This couldn't be real, It couldn't be. tears welled in my eyes and my breathing jolted into hyperventilating as I turned to see the opening of the edge of the cliff.

What took place before me was what I was desperately crying to not be real.

"NO! Wait!" I ran towards him- my bleeding, barely conscious legend of a father- laying at the edge of the cliff. There must've been seven- no- ten gargoyles there. I yelled, gripping my sword so tightly that my knuckles turned white. Charging at them full speed, I did everything I was trained to do, and more. The panic and the fear left instantly, replaced by rage. I swung in every direction, staying on my guard, slicing and turning at every gargoyle in my path. They stabbed me, scratched me, and hit me. I didn't care, the adrenaline that rampaged through my body kept me from feeling anything but fear and fury.

But I had taken too long.

Slowly, the anger dissipated, turning into sorrow and disbelief. I kneeled to his side and held his head.

"Dad?" If he didn't respond I might've screamed right then and there. "You're okay, you're fine." Tears just flowed. They came like a waterfall, blurring my vision. I tried so hard to steady my hand while holding his head. My other hand shakily pressed my sleeve against the deep gash in his chest, now understanding why they make our coats red.

"Nedrall," He breathed. "Listen to me." I didn't interrupt him. I didn't know how much time he had left. "They're not here for us. They're here for the girl. The ghost. You are a Nutcracker. You're more like that girl than you know, but you are and always will be my boy."

My boy. He always would call me his boy. I always wanted to be just like him and he always believed I would be better than him. I remembered sitting on a rug every night. The fireplace was always lit. He was always wearing a sweater. There was always a bedtime story.

I remembered the stories of the days of General Nutcracker and Commander Aidan. 'The Nutcracker', as they called him, had slain the mouse king. He saved the love of his life, and was supposed to live happily ever after. That happily ever after was being stolen from him. From me.

I didn't really process what he said at the time. I was scared.

He continued. "Tell Aidan to protect that girl." He tried to bring his hand to my face, but didn't have the strength. I held it there for him.

"Don't leave me here, please." I cried. "I can't- you can't leave me!" I was trembling, cold, and broken.

He became still.

I moved my hand from his face to his neck. There was nothing. His hand dropped from my face. I had so much more to tell him, we had so much more to do, he had so much more to teach me. It's not fair. He wasn't done living yet.

"No! No, no, no, no, no," I pressed my forehead to his chest, and shut my eyes. I just wanted to dissapear. He was soaked with blood. His blood. My blood.

"NO!" I finally screamed. I screamed it out for the world to hear, gargoyles and humans alike. It echoed through the woods and I gripped his hand. I sobbed, and sobbed. Not a minute later, I heard a voice behind me.

"Ned?" It was a woman's voice. I recognized it immediately. It had changed- matured- ever so slightly. But the soft echo and gentleness sounded otherworldly. I turned.

"You? Why are you here now? Why didn't you do anything?" She's the Christmas Spirit, I remembered that much. Why didn't she do anything to help?

"I am so sorry, I could not get here in time." Tears welled in her eyes. "He saw me earlier, and he told me to run. He said that it was very important that I find you again but he didn't tell me why."

"Well he told me to protect you and to take you to General Aidan. He said that the gargoyles are here for you." I didn't want to believe that she had led them here, to us. It didn't seem like something the spirit I met before would do. "Why did you lead them here?"

"They cornered me- their army was much larger than anything I had seen before- and I had nowhere else to go." She seemed to hug herself, and wouldn't make eye contact with me.

My eyes were still red and wet with tears. I was exhausted, and wanted all of this to be over. I just wanted the nightmare to end.

"We need to get out of here." I sighed and rubbed my eyes, preparing myself to look back down at him. I stood up, and took a deep breath. I didn't want to turn around. When I did, tears flooded from my eyes in amounts more than I even thought was possible.. I picked him up, sighing shakily. quietly, Carol rested her hand on my shoulder, it felt as if a warm campfire had been placed there. Her hand was so warm and comforting that my head instinctively leaned against it- hoping that the sharp numbness in my cheek would go away.

"I really, truly am sorry. I wish I could've done more." She whispered.

"Me too."

She let go, and I turned to walk back the way I came from. She followed behind silently.

A scratchy noise beeped through the walkie-talkie that hung from my belt.

"What is that?" Carol picked up the old walkie-talkie carefully.

"Oh, that's just-"

"Please pick up! Comet! Please tell me you're hearing this!" Charles' voice came through it.

I whipped around to face her. "Press the green button," I ordered Carol. She looked confused but did it anyway.

"Addams, I'm safe. I-" How was I supposed to tell him about this? "Where are you? I'll be slow getting back, there's three of us."

"Three? Did Paris find you?"

"Uhm, no," I responded shakily. "I.. I.." I swallowed my tears. I dreaded having to say it out loud. "I'm carrying my dad." Tears continued to well in my eyes.

It was silent for a moment. I took a deep, trembling breath.

"What? Is he okay?" Charles asked softly. My dad was as much of a parent to him as he was to me.

"He's gone," I finally admitted. "I didn't get to him fast enough and now he's gone."

From what I could hear, it sounded like Charles dropped the walkie-talkie, and someone else had picked it up. Carol looked like she might cry with me.

"It is my fault," She started. "I am the reason the gargoyles are here. I came here because I thought it would be safe."

"Who is that? Is there a girl with you?" Dante's voice came through.

"Yeah,." I sighed, looking at Carol. "I have the Christmas Spirit with me."

"Oh, wow." Dante said. In the silence that followed, I tried to find a way to continue talking without talking about the enormous elephant in the room.

I wanted to be done talking. I really just wanted to be alone, but with Carol it felt different. It felt like I was alone with her. "Is Fayola okay?."

"She's alright, luckily, the trees broke most of her fall. Unfortunately, the trees broke most of her legs." Dante answered. I could tell he was trying to shove all the elephants out of the room with humor.

"Alright. Over and out." I spoke to the walkie-talkie numbly.

"Over and out." Dante replied, disheartened.

Carol and I continued walking through the woods in silence. I heard a beep or buzz or static every now and then and I didn't know if it was someone trying to reach me through the walkie-talkie, or if it was Carol messing with it. Frankly, in the moment I didn't care.

A few minutes of walking later, I heard the clopping of hooves through snow.

"Nutcracker!" I heard Commander Packer shout.

"If you can hear us, say something!" General Aidan followed up.

I assumed they weren't looking for me.

"Over here! We're here!" I shouted to them anyway, turning to the direction of the clatter.

"This way!" I heard General Aidan say to the commanders.

I was going to have to say it again. My dad is dead. I had to be the one to tell everyone. For some reason they all had to hear it from me. They started to approach and I didn't say anything, I just looked at the ground.

"Cadet Nutcracker, what's going on? What happened?" Aidan asked me, sliding off his horse. I just looked at him, not knowing what to say. He looked at me, then at Carol, then at dad. "What-"

"I'm sorry." I squeaked. I forced back my tears. "I tried so hard, I did." Aidan took him from my arms.. I had to take a breath when he did. My father's blood stained most of my arms and abdomen at this point.

"He told me, before he died, to bring the Christmas Spirit to you, because we have to keep her safe. They're after her, not us. They followed her and she was in the wrong place at the wrong time. But none of this is her fault, she thought she would be safe here."

Carol turned to me when I said that, with an expression of surprise and gratefulness.

Commander Woodlaine slid off of their horse and walked firmly towards me. I held my breath, believing she was going to yell at Carol for not saving him in time. Instead they hugged me. Tight, around my neck. I hugged them back, noticing the blood transfer onto their uniform.

"It's not your fault, I'm so sorry, Ned." They cooed.

"And... that's her?" He asked, looking at Carol. There was an unfamiliar weakness to his voice that I was sure no one had ever heard before.

"Yes. This is the Christmas Spirit. Her name is Carol." I introduced.

"I am so sorry for bringing this trouble here and all the damage I have caused." Carol apologized.

I nervously awaited General Aidan's response. There was no way to tell how he'd react.

"This isn't your fault. It's not your fault they attack us." Commander Woodlaine spoke. "They probably want her for her magic. If they can get a hold of spirit magic they'll be able to use it to enhance their own magic. If that happens-"

"They'll be unstoppable." General Aidan finished their sentence. He sighed, looking at Carol, then at my dad, then at me. "They've already retreated, and now I know why. Let's get you two inside. We'll deal with this later."

General Adian's horse kneeled and he mounted it, my father still limp in his arms. I mounted General Aidan's horse behind him and Carol rode back with Commander Woodlaine.

On the way back, I could've sworn I saw a tear roll down Aidan's cheek.

Four

Next In Line, Please

When we arrived back at base, my team was there waiting for me. Paris stood with Dante and Fayola, who sat uncomfortably in a wheelchair, and Charles didn't wait for us to enter the gates before he started running to us. Dante's arms wrapped around himself like a hug, and he looked at me with pity in his eyes. After we went through the gates, I dropped from General Aidan's horse and Charles hugged me, practically catching me on the way down. He started to weep. My eyes were red and puffy, the cold stung worse than it ever had before. I felt like I'd ran out of tears to cry. I hugged him back, not needing to speak a word. After he let go, he wiped his eyes and started to walk back. Before I knew it, Carol was walking next to me too. We had a team group hug rather than a team huddle like everyone else was doing. I needed a hug a lot more than I wanted to talk to anyone.

We walked as a group to the mess hall, our heads hanging in defeat while everyone went on in excitement about our so-called victory. They were all eating dinner when I got back. How could I eat after all of that? I walked with the others as they got their food, and we sat isolated at a table in the corner of the Mess Hall

I overheard others talking as they passed by us, carrying their food.

They talked about how it was our most successful encounter with Gargoyles yet.

They said that there were no casualties.

"I feel... out of place." Carol poked at her food with the wrong end of a fork. "I don't know where I'm supposed to go." I didn't know where they planned to keep Carol either, or if they planned to keep her here at all.

"We'll take you over to General Aidan when we're done here." Dante told her.

"General Codagh would probably be a better bet, right? Because General Aidan's probably not... in the best mood." Paris spoke up.

"Yeah," I agreed, not taking my eyes off the table. "I can take you now, since I'm not eating."

The group sat in silence, neither agreeing or disagreeing. I realized that they were just shocked that I was saying anything at all.

"Alright." Carol pushed back her chair and hopped up. I stood up after she did, and we started walking to the Generals' Cabin. I noticed that Carol kept looking at the side of my head.

"Your ear- I almost forgot about that incident." She tilted her head, gazing at the scar.

"Yeah, it scarred over, thankfully."

"That day, why were you out there? Alone in the woods... during an ambush."

"I was looking for you, actually. It's... ironic. I went there with Charles. Everything seemed fine at the time- I guess it was a surprise attack?" Carol was successful in distracting me from my own thoughts.

"There is something I didn't tell you... in the woods. It didn't feel like the right time." Carol stopped walking, fiddling with her hands.

I stopped walking, and turned to face her. "What?"I dreaded her response, desperately wishing that nothing else would happen that night or ever again. And she was right, it was definitely the wrong time to talk about whatever she was about to tell me. The whole situation still felt unreal.

"Ya know what? Don't even tell me. I just-" I let out a tired, frustrated sigh and ran my hands back through my hair. "Everything's going really fast right now. We'll talk about it after all of *this* is dealt with." It wasn't my intention to sound blunt, but I didn't have the energy to care. I was exhausted.

"You're... right. Let's keep walking" She apologized, hanging her head.

We kept walking, the awkward silence hung over us noticeably. The blank tan walls and wood tiled floors seemed to go on forever. Walking in an endless uncomfortable silence down an empty, dull hallway. I thought about where she would be staying, I didn't know of any protocol for housing a not-actually-mythical mythical being. Who knows, maybe there was one, today was full of surprises anyways.

Finally, we approached General Codagh's cabin. As the E.L.F. General, she basically lives in a warehouse. They say that no one that's camped around here gets any sleep with the screeches and clanking that's always coming from inside. Now I knew what they meant. I knocked, but I wasn't sure if she would hear me through all the mechanical nonsense going on in there. Before anyone could answer the door, Carol raised her head with concern.

"Wait, they do not think that I am the one who did that, do they?" She stammered, her eyes lighting up with worry. I didn't have to ask what it was that they thought she did.

"No, they know it was a gargoyle."

I wanted to get all of the talking about it over with, I wanted everything to go back to normal. But every memory, every sinking, exhausted, aggrieved feeling that was sinking down my chest knew that wasn't ever going to happen. I already hated talking about it and not even a day had passed.

The heavy metallic creaking of General Codagh's door distracted me, and I jumped a little at the loud noise.

"Ah, hello, Cadet." Codagh peeked through the ajar door. "And company." She added, noticing Carol. "Come on in, what's on yer mind?" General Codagh was a nutjob for sure, but still, she was gentle. I walked in to see some machine sitting on a large table, and in front of it was a rolling chair surrounded by other tables stacked to the brim with what I could only assume were explosives that should not be stored as carelessly as they were.

"Afternoon General, Carol and I came to ask where she'd be staying. Sorry for coming now, I can see you're busy, I just wasn't sure how much free time there was after supper." Despite my exhaustion, I stood as straight as I could and spoke with more respect than I had for anyone at that moment.

Carol bowed, her hair falling off of her back in front of her shoulders and folded her hands. "I am sorry for all of the trouble and hassle I've caused." As General Codagh and I watched her, I noticed that she must've slipped off her boots while I was talking. My eyes moved from her bare feet to the door, where her boots lay, the top of it falling over the other one, leaning to one side.

"It's not your fault that they're after ya, kid. And yeah, we can figure somethin' out for ya. Paris was on yer team today right?" She asked me. "She was there when we arrived back at the gate, so..." Codagh paused, slightly furrowing her brow and rubbing her face in thought. "Yeah, you buddy up with Paris for now, a'ight?"

Carol straightened her posture again, dropping her shoulders. "Yes ma'am. Thank you very much." She closed her hands together and bowed slightly again.

"No problem, darlin'. I'll be seein' ya." General Codagh started to usher us out of the room. "Get to ye quarters now, dinner's 'bout over. And get some good rest. Unfortunately, we don't get breaks, even after battle."

Work. Of course I had to work. I thought maybe Aidan would give us both a day off, but that man would probably continue to work if he had a sword sticking out of his chest.

"Thank you." I waved as we exited the room. On the way back down the hall, the silence lingered over us like a thundercloud.

"I do not think you should work tomorrow." Carol announced, raising her chin up.

"I don't even think General Aidan wants to work tomorrow. He was a commander under my dad before he became General. They were really close, my dad taught him everything he knows. They both taught me everything I know. I don't think General Aidan would stop working even if he wanted to, though."

"Why is that?" Carol inquired.

"He's the General. He doesn't get a day off, even to mourn. Hell, we should be celebrating today. Not one person died except for him; everything went perfectly right except for that. It just doesn't make sense. It's not fair." I said, becoming progressively more frustrated.

"You are right," Carol agreed. "And for what it is worth," She placed her hand gently on my back. "You have done the best work today out of any soldier I have ever seen."

Eventually, we got back to the table, where everyone had finished eating. Carol explained to Paris that she'd stay in her dorm.

"Oh, ok! We actually don't have a lot of people in our room, so no worries!" Paris responded, even though Carol wasn't worried about that at all. After Paris and Carol left, Dante started talking. "Have you talked to General Aidan yet?"

"No, I'll probably catch him tomorrow. Everyone's tired right now, anyways." I answered more gloomily than I had intended.

Charles cut in: "Yeah. We ain't gotta think about what comes next yet." He walked next to me and hugged me from the side, patting my back. "One step at a time, Comet."

Silently, Fayola held my hand. This was the only time I'd ever physically look down at Fayola, which would have made me laugh if I wasn't so fatigued. Instead I smiled at her.

Dante pulled both Charles and I into a hug, and Fay was still holding my hand.

"We should get to bed. All of us." Dante notioned. We all nodded in agreement. Charles left silently, rubbing his eyes and taking deep breaths, a telltale sign that he was barring his emotions for later. Fayola grabbed both of our hands and squeezed them tightly. Dante and I had started to head back to our room when he sighed and rolled his head back.

"I swear, if Tyler and company have anything smart to say I'm gonna knock his teeth out." He growled.

"I don't really care what he has to say at this point." I replied.

"Alright, but don't take any shit. It's like my dad always told me: if they serve it out, dish it back!"

I appreciated the effort.

I sighed and opened the door to our room, and everyone else was already inside. They were enthusiastically talking about all the cool things they did during the battle. They continued their conversation as we sat on our beds.

One of the twins sliced off a gargoyle's whole wing, and the other had shot two gargoyles down with one arrow.

Tyler was battered and bloody. He talked about how he got into a fistfight with a gargoyle twice his size and escaped.

"What'd you two do today?" Asam asked, gesturing to Dante and I.

"Yeah, Nutcracker, you look bloodied up." Basil added.

"It's not mine." I answered, not bothering to look at them as I tucked my gear under the bed.

"What, daddy didn't come to the rescue?" Tyler snarled.

"Shut your fuckin' mouth, Tyler," Dante stood up and was in Tyler's face the millisecond he finished his sentence.

My sword was still in my grip, and I was about to put it away before Tyler decided to open his mouth. I walked over to him and Dane backed up. Holding my sword up next to his chin, I spoke: "I don't give one single shit about your daddy issues, Tyler. It's not my problem, so don't make it mine. And for your fucking information, I watched my father die in my arms today. So if I were you, I'd shut the hell up and learn how to use a sword before it kills you."

I backed off and put my sword under my bed.

The next morning, I felt like I was tied down to my bed with heavy steel chains. After a few minutes, I finally pulled myself out of bed and got ready. My eyes were less red now, and less swollen-looking. Dante informed me that Tyler left before I woke up. Before I left, Asam put his hand on my shoulder.

"I'm sorry for your loss, man. His legacy will never die, ever." He consoled me.

I nodded. "Thank you, it means a lot to me." I answered with a generic response.

After I left, I started towards the T.O.Y. HQ. I walked quickly to avoid being told by every other person how great of a man my dad was. I assumed everyone around me knew and was staring. I felt eyes burning into me, eyes that I wasn't even 100 percent sure were there. I just kept my head down and kept walking.

A few seconds passed of me not being sure if someone was actually calling my name or not until I turned around to look.

"Nutcracker! Stop walking so fast, kid, geez." It was Commander Woodlaine.

I stopped in my tracks. "Commander?" I looked at them with confusion. "Is there an issue?"

"No, just-" She stopped a few feet away from me. "General Aidan wants to speak with you."

"Is he in his office, Commander?" I asked, fixing my posture.

"No. He's in the Royal Courtyard with King Klaus. Since we're stationed so close to the capitol he stays close to the King at all times." Commander Woodlaine spouted.

"Why's that?" I inquired.

"You serious? They're like two peas in a pod. Inseparable even."

"Really?" There weren't two personalities more polar opposite than King Klaus' and Aidan's. "Huh."

"Yeah, unlikely for sure, but they make a great team. Now get goin', Cadet." Commander Woodlaine ordered before walking away.

"Sir, yes sir. Thank you, Commander." After parting ways, I darted towards the courtyard, understanding General Aidan's impatience.

When I finally reached the courtyard, I had to navigate around the fountain to be able to even see the doors to the throne room. The palace was like something out of a fairytale- everything was carved out of marble, silver, and gold. Huge marble pillars supported the silver canopy that stretched back unnecessarily far to reach the wall. I marched up the stairs, my boots stomping quickly the whole way. At the end of the stairs was an extensive pathway to the door to the throne room. The door was enormous, much larger than even King Klaus. If the whole place wasn't powered by the King's magic the doors would probably take a dozen people to open. It was shaped like an arch, with beautiful golden arches that crawled up the sides like rose vines. Ironically enough, the door had handles that were made of silver.

I knocked, and it barely sounded like a click against the monstrous door. I knocked again, harder this time, pounding my fist against it three times. The door seemed to glitter and shine with gold as it opened on King Klaus' command.

I entered the throne room, and was met with a velvet-red rug beneath my feet that led to the throne, where King Klaus sat. Instinctively, I kneeled and bowed my head. In training, we were told we must always bow in the presence of the king, even though he had known me since I was a kid.

"No, No, stand up boy, no need for that here." King Klaus spoke, his voice booming through the room like a cathedral. The King's throne room was a large, golden cupola. Three arched frames that supported its structure stood tall and glistening. Between each frame was a painting of the symbols representing each branch of our military on a crimson background. None of them was bigger or more grand than the other, none of them more emphasized. One section had a silver shield, with bronze colored spears lined up horizontally behind it. This represented the leaders of the T.O.Y. workforce. The T.O.Y. General was the shield, and each spear was one of the three commanders. In the next section, there was a shiny metal cog. The gear gleamed in three different ends, again, representing the General and Commanders of the E.L.F. branch. In the last part, there was an open map, with dashes, lines, and markings of landmarks and buildings. It was a map of our kingdom. There were walls separating each section of the kingdom, it was separated into fourths, the capitol was at one end, and at each of the other three ends were towers. This map symbolized the I.M.P. branch: Internal Military

Police. An unfortunate acronym but apparently that was the best they could come up with.

As I stood back up, I faced General Aidan. "General Aidan, sir." I saluted.

"Cadet Nutcracker," Aidan acknowledged, looking up at King Klaus, who was sitting on his throne. "I called you here to discuss memorial service arrangements." he looked back at me. Aidan started to fiddle with his hands, then put them behind his back.

"Right, um," I didn't know what to say or do. I'd never had to deal with this before. I knew joining the military would be a reality check, but this felt like a reality punch in the face. "I would like to hold it as soon as possible. After we release the news of his death to the public is when I want to hold the service."

"Alright." Aidan swallowed. "Then we will tell the press today. They've already been asking us about the outcome of the battle, and we wanted to wait for your opinion."

"Allow us to talk with the press, we will call you if you are asked to show, and it will be completely up to you whether or not you want to talk with the press." King Klaus affirmed. "Take today off, son, go home for a few days."

"You have the rest of this week to take for yourself." Aidan added.

"Thank you, sir. But if I may," I spoke, remembering Charles the previous night. "I would request that you let Cadet Charles Addams off as well. He was just as close to my father as I was."

Aidan sighed, almost as if annoyed, but his face was understanding. "Yes. He may go with you. You are dismissed, Nutcracker."

"Thank you, sir." I saluted both of them, and marched out of the King's throne room. When I was no longer in sight of either of them, I went back on my way to my room, taking out my walkie-talkie to inform Charles.

"Addams? We're off for the rest of this week. I'm heading home, I suggest you do the same. Over."

I packed my bag up and left through the capitol base gates. I was still in uniform when I called a carriage over to lend me a ride a few blocks away. I didn't live very far from the capitol, because of my dad being a General. Generals always stay close to the capitol because that's where they work in peacetime. During the ride, I dreaded how empty my home would feel now. For the last 24 hours I wanted nothing more than to go home, but now that I was, I felt sick to my stomach. I'd stayed home alone for weeks before, not knowing if my dad was going to come back. But he did every time. I couldn't decide what hurt more: knowing he wasn't coming home or not knowing anything. The carriage stopped, and I stepped down onto the road. By that time, Charles came back on the walkie-talkie.

"Thanks for the relay, are you at Navid's house? Over."

"Yeah." I responded to the walkie. "You comin' here? Over."

"Yup, on my way. Over and out."

I could feel my heart jumping through my chest as I approached my house. The door waited for me menacingly, its pale blue surface had been repainted one too many times. The wreath that hung on it year-round had also been replaced often. Even though we had to switch the dead one for a new one, its green pine-tree leaves always swirled the same way and the pine cones were always placed in the same spot.

Slowly, I opened the door.

I walked slowly through my living room, the house that I grew up in, the house that was so lively and full of color now felt gray and monochrome. I felt like a ghost, spectating the past. My boots treaded over the old cranberry-colored rug that I used to sit on when he told me stories, but grew too tough to be comfortable. We never replaced it because it was hand-made, and stitched into it was his greatest achievement, defeating the Mouse King. I sat my walkie on the side table next to the couch. On the other side of the couch was a hallway that led to my old room. He kept my room the same after I moved out and went to boot camp.

"Why would we need another guest room? The only people that come over here are you, Aidan and Addams!" He always told me. The hallway was unnecessarily long, nothing hung on the bare beige walls. Because my room was at the end of the hall, I had to walk past the bathroom on my left, broom closet on my right, then the guest room was on the left, directly facing my room. Going into my bedroom, it looked more like a museum than how it would've actually looked when I was a child. The bed was made, every book was lined up on the shelf and there wasn't a speck of dust anywhere, even on the toy chest that remained at the foot of my bed. My bed extended from the left wall of the room, in the middle. There seemed to be a hundred blankets and pillows on it, even though I only ever slept with one of each. At the farthest wall stood my old wardrobe. Upon further inspection I learned that it was empty, all of my old clothes were most likely in chests in the attic. My old desk sat in the far right corner, where I remembered drawing out a map of the forest that I found Carol in. I decided to leave everything where it was and went back to the living room. Looking at the rug again, the gears in my head started to turn.

There was no way that my father being the only death in that battle was a coincidence.

I started to connect the dots. It wasn't an accident or a coincidence at all. No, they wouldn't leak surprise attack information that quickly, and if they did, why would they continue to go through with the plan?

When an unknown threat occurs, some veterans are asked to come back and help.

They must've wanted him to come back.

The room started to spin around me. I sat on the couch and rubbed my hand across my face, furrowing my eyebrows in thought. My mind spiraled deep into thought. Why would they go after a veteran? Even being the threat my father was, he wasn't fighting anymore, so why would they target him? Was I overthinking this? I leaned against the wall, contemplating the legitimacy of gargoyles strategically bringing a veteran back into the field just to target him. Then I heard a familiar jingle of windchimes. The screen door squeaked open, and Charles walked through.

"Charles they targeted him." I spouted, not knowing for sure if this was true myself.

"What?" Charles said confusedly as the door closed behind him.

"They faked a surprise attack to get veterans back in the field just to target him."

Charles' face looked as if he'd been told that all frogs had two legs. "Slow down, explain. Why would they target a veteran if they're already retired?"

"That's what I'm trying to figure out." The more I thought about it, the more I panicked. I was already expected to not work for the rest of the week, how was I supposed to hold this information for a week?

"Ned," Charles repeated. "Slow. Down." He grabbed my arms, which were folded on top of each other. "Take it easy for now, okay? We have a bit more to think about right now."

He was right. I had a memorial service to plan. fun.

I sighed. "Okay, what do we do now, then? King Klaus and General Aidan told me that they'd call me and tell me about interviewing the press, and we agreed that we'd hold a public memorial after it became public knowledge."

"Okay." He let go of my arms.

"I really don't want to do interviews."

"I know." Charles sighed, shakily. He stood next to me, also leaning against the wall. "Woodlaine told me to tell you to pick out the clothes he'll wear for the service, so let's start there."

I could feel my breath shake, so I held it. I could feel tears rising, so I closed my eyes. How many more times did I have to break down until I felt normal again?

I couldn't see him, but I felt Charles hug me, and I felt him shaking as well. I opened my eyes to see his coily pinkish hair, the side of his head against me in the hug.

"I know this is the hardest thing you've ever done, but I'll be damned if you do it alone. We just have to keep picking each other up and pushing through. We can get through this together." Charles cried through shaky breaths.

I pulled him into the hug tighter.

"It's you and me, even if it's just us for the rest of time, I won't let you go. You're my best friend." I cried.

I stood up, and he backed off of the hug. We were both bawling like newborn babies.

"If we have to do all this, we're having it done right. I'm tired of *wanting* someone to tell me what to do or where to go, I'm tired of being lost." I declared, looking at my father in the rug, who held his chin high and his sword higher.

"Damn straight." Charles replied. I couldn't help but giggle a bit.

Still crying, we marched into my father's room, and went through his closet together. We went through his uniforms, his suits, and his normal clothes, and we decided that he should wear his favorite sweater. His sash and uniform, along with all of his medals and awards would be kept at a memorial museum for all of the fallen heroes in this long war. He always told everyone that no one- whether they were a general, Cadet, or commander- was better than the other. When we finished, the home phone started to ring. Charles picked it up first, and received the times and dates of interviews.

The next few days went as expected. interviews, newspapers, letters, and more interviews. They asked about everything, more than anyone should even want to know about my father and I. They asked about his favorite foods, drinks, games, shows, books. They asked about his love life, they asked about *my* love life: no comment. They asked about hobbies and medals, they asked what my plan was going forward.

no comment.

On Saturday morning, I woke up to see my dad's front yard flooded with people, flowers, signs, and candles, among other things. I quickly made myself presentable before I stepped foot outside. I still had pajamas on, but I didn't really mind. Neither did everyone else.

Charles and Paris approached me when I stepped off the porch.

"What's going on?" I asked, pretending that their commotion didn't wake me up at noon.

"Surprise!" Paris said, wrapping her arms around me in a quick hug. "The team and this community wanted to do something special on our own before the service tomorrow."

"Who all was in on this?" I said, waving to all the people on the street.

"Everyone. Except for you, of course." Charles answered, pulling his signature long glove back up his arm.

We walked down to meet Dante and Fayola, who immediately greeted me with hugs and tea that Fayola had brought. I talked to all of the people, and it felt similar to an interview, but it was one that I actually enjoyed. So many different signs read praises of me and my father: "The Nutcracker heroes!" "Hero Navid Nutcracker!" "General Nutcracker: War Hero and Father!"

Looking farther down the street, I saw General Aidan and Commander Woodlaine approach us from the sidewalk. If I knew they'd be here I wouldn't have worn pajamas. I mentally prepared myself for the following conversation with a swig of Fayola's tea and fake confidence.

"Morning, General." I said, trying not to laugh at myself when I realized that my team was laughing at me too.

"Morning. One hell of a way to wake up, huh?" Aidan said. I tried to avoid the fact that his eyes were red and sore-looking.

"Sure is." I responded.

"A celebration of life!" Woodlaine laughed heartily. Aidan rolled his eyes.

"Yes sir!" Dante agreed.

"While I didn't come here to talk about work," Aidan started, "When you return to base on monday, there's a gargoyle we need you to identify. She says she's a spy, and that she's met you before." He glanced at my ear- or lack thereof.

"Oh- alrig-" I caught myself. "Yes Sir."

"Don't rush. We have time, and she's in containment." Aidan told me.

"Honestly, she's been the easiest gargoyle to work with. She's calm, and very willing to compromise. Hell, she acts more like our ally than our enemy." Woodlaine added.

"A gargoyle betraying gargoyles? Has that ever happened before?" Paris asked.

"It hasn't." Aidan answered.

"Well," I said, trying to change the subject, "What do we do now?"

"Send everyone home, I guess." Dante looked out into the street.

It had been at least thirty minutes since they got here, and their arms looked tired. They blew out their candles and Dante, Fay, and Paris ushered them down the sidewalk. I waved my team goodbye and then It was just me, Charles, Aidan, and Woodlaine left.

"General Aidan, spars are today." Came Commander Packer's voice through Aidan's radio. "In case you forgot. Over."

General Aidan rolled his eyes as he held his mic to respond. "Hold your tongue Commander. I'm on my way." He looked at Woodlane. "We oughta get back to the arena before Packer and Manning have to do anything by themselves."

"I'll be right behind ya, gimme a minute or two." Woodlaine responded.

"Please don't leave me with them, Woods." Aidan groaned sarcastically.

"You got this, I won't take long." Woodlaine laughed.

"Don't keep them long, Nutcracker. They have work to do." He said, pointing to Woodlaine.

"Yes sir." I saluted. Aidan grabbed the attention of a carriage and he went on his way, press and fans trying to run after him.

"Alrighty." Commander Woodlaine turned to me. "Listen, Cadet. I'm sorry for your loss, I really am. I know this is gonna affect how you think in the future."

"I know."

"But listen, Aidan's the same way."

I was confused. "What do you mean?"

"General Aidan's got anxiety. It affects his performance on the battlefield sometimes, which is why I'm his commander. teammates help each other out." Woodlaine put their hand on my shoulder. "You've got a team, Nutcracker. People are in your corner, and so am I, alright?"

"Yes Commander. Thank you." I reached up and rubbed their hand and just as soon as everyone arrived, Woodlaine patted my back and hopped on a carriage back to the base.

I went back to my porch, where some people had left their posters and candles. I blew out their candles and took the signs inside, placing them on the couch. The next day was the day of the funeral, and because our family wasn't extensive at all, there wasn't going to be a personal family service. If we did that, it probably would just be Charles, Aidan, and myself. I had a speech prepared, but I also felt like I shouldn't just stick to the outline. I've always been the type of person to need a plan, but something felt different this time.

Five

Jeez, Who Died?

I found myself sprinting through the woods. I knew I was running from something but from what I wasn't sure. My sword was drawn, and bloody. In full uniform I sprinted through the snow, leaving behind bloody footprints. I couldn't tell if it was mine or not. Every time my foot hit the ground I felt like I was running slower and slower, and my breathing became shorter. I heard explosions and bombs behind me. Their light made the snow on the trees ahead of me flash warmly with yellow. The pounding of my heart and the bomb's roars filled my ear until I couldn't even hear myself breathe. Faintly, I could hear the combined screams of my team. I wasn't sure what was happening or where I was, the burning fear in my chest kept me from turning around. Tears fell one by one out of my eyes- the sharp wind stabbed at them like a thousand needles.

I shot up in a cold sweat. 4:46 a.m. My uniform hanging on my closet door shimmered softly in the moonlight. My eyes darted around. It was my father's room.

I took a few deep breaths to myself, understanding that I'd probably woken up from a nightmare. Figuring there was no reason to go back to sleep now, I got out of the bed and made my way through the darkness to the light switch. Upon flicking it, I saw that the bed was in shambles.

Pillows were on the floor, scattered amongst thrown blankets. I decided to leave it be and go make coffee. I tried to remember what my nightmare was about, but failed to do so. I had about six hours before the memorial service at 11:00. It felt too quiet, so I turned on my dad's busted old radio. Today's morning news wasn't playing this early so I listened to yesterday's evening news.

The voice on the radio spoke: "Tomorrow at the Golden Gates Plaza just one block from the Capitol steps, there will be Former-General and war hero Navid Nutcracker's memorial service. General Aidan, King Klaus, and Navid's son, who is a Cadet serving in the T.O.Y. Workforce will be speaking. King Klaus will be the first to speak at 11:00 am."

As the coffee pot started to brew, I listened to two people on the radio discuss my father's achievements and how sudden and tragic it was. It was nothing I hadn't heard before, but I stopped to listen when they started talking about me.

"Now, his son, Nedrall, has only been in the workforce for what? A month maybe? And how everything went down; that hits hard." spoke the first man.

"He basically started at the top of his food chain," Spoke a woman's voice. "After going through something like that... It's impossible to tell him he doesn't deserve to be there."

"You think he's listening to this?"

"No, I'm sure he has better things to do."

"If he is though- which he probably isn't listening- I'd tell him that the whole kingdom's got his back. He's gonna do great things, I tell ya."

"Definitely, even at the rally around his house this morning, I was there, he seemed delighted. He even looked like he was talking business with his team and General Aidan as well."

"Say what you like about the kid, but he sure ain't a quitter."

Ironic: that would be my favorite thing to do at the moment. But I knew I couldn't sulk anymore, not after Charles' ramble the other day.

The coffee pot finished rumbling, and I stopped listening to the radio long enough to grab a mug from the cupboard. By the time I was drinking my coffee, the radio had changed subject to the weather for today. They said It'd be a nice sunny day, with a light breeze and not too hot. A perfect summer day. The index cards that sat neatly at the corner of the counter was my speech. It was less of a whole speech and more of notes that I wanted to talk about. I set down my half-empty coffee cup to go over them for the ten-billionth time. After I'd finished going over what I'd say, I finished my coffee. Now it was 5:30. I knew that Paris, Fayola, and Dante's alarms were going off. Charles was probably taking the break opportunity to sleep as much as possible. Breaks this long happened very seldom so it was best to take what you could get.

I guess my brain wasn't allowing me that break. For that whole week, I'd woken up at various hours of the night in a panic.

After an hour or two of cleaning up the house, because what else did I have to do, the phone started ringing. It hung on the wall right under the clock in the kitchen. When I picked it up, Paris was on the other side.

"Hello?" I said.

"Hey Ned! Uh, We're all gonna be at the service today. Like, the team. You know what I mean." Paris responded, sounding out of breath. "I can't talk right now though, Codagh says she's gonna whip us into shape, cuz that's definitely not what we spent four years at boot camp for, bye!"

Before I could respond, the phone hung up. I couldn't help but laugh. Paris always sounds rushed, like she's always coming up with an excuse or lying on the spot like a middle schooler who forgot the homework was due today.

The rest of that morning was spent distracting myself and going over my notes again. I went grocery shopping, but I got the cart with the messed up wheel, so I just rolled the cart at a specific angle so it wasn't too loud. My nerves started to increase in tension more and more as the hours passed. I knew I had memorized my cards, but I went over them anyways because what if I didn't remember something? Deeper into the rabbit hole I went, continuing my thoughts on 'Why'. Why him? I felt confident in the theory of the gargoyles just wanted to spread fear, but something else was off. There weren't very many injuries at all in the battle, and Fayola was among the worst with two broken legs, so what was going on?

Maybe that other gargoyle had something to do with it. I remembered her long, jet black hair, purple horns that split her bangs into three sections. They twisted around each other like vines and met at the tip. I suppose she could use them for impaling even though most gargoyles used their horns to catch people's swords in them.

That gargoyle was probably the one Aidan brought in, and she must have some type of charm about her if General Aidan let her in. There was something so blurrily familiar about her, though I couldn't put my finger on it.

Before I knew it, it was 10:30, and I hopped on a carriage to the Plaza. General Aidan and the commanders were all there. King Klaus was there as well, greeting the people below the stage. The only proper way to describe the King was astronomical. He made Fayola look short in a side-by-side comparison. I had no idea what his exact height was, but he was definitely huge. I stepped down from the carriage and quickly made my way to the Plaza stage, going to meet up with General Aidan. With a quick glance over the crowd, I noticed Fayola right away. Standing with her was the rest of the team.

"Aye, son, how are ya doin'?" Commander Manning saw me first.

"I'm doing better, thanks." I spoke, not knowing whether or not the Commanders expected me to address them formally. All four of their facial expressions told me that I was fine.

Aidan's eyes were still red. Mine were still red as well, and as we looked at each other I felt a closer understanding between us.

Awkward hugs went around the group until King Klaus joined us, practically picking up both me and General Aidan. With his presence, the air suddenly felt lighter.

"Well don't suffocate 'em," Commander Packer laughed. "If they can't breathe they won't be able to speak!"

King Klaus let us down with a hearty laugh. "I know they'll do just fine!"

Aidan adjusted his uniform. "Well, it wouldn't be the first time I'd have to give a speech unprepared." Aidan snapped, rolling his eyes.

Commander Woodlain giggled. "You still upset about the opening ceremony?"

"Yes, in fact. Crixus was the one meant to give that speech. He's lucky I'm the only one who remembered the speech." Aidan said.

"Ah, you'll be alright," Commander Woodlaine looked down at their watch and their face turned to surprise. "Ope, King, It's about time you got to the stage sir!"

"Yes it is," He agreed, turning his head to look at the crowd around the curtain. King Klaus turned back to us, waved, and headed to the stand.

The stand was small compared to him, but stood averagely next to someone my size. It was wooden, and tapestries of the symbols of each branch hung on the front. it rose from the ground in almost a trapezoidal shape, with a microphone and binder on top that was full of papers. Everyone stopped talking as the King approached the stand.

"Citizens of Takkochsivy, today we give tribute to a fallen hero." As he spoke, the four of us went behind the stage. The King's voice was still very prominent, even from other rooms. Though the microphone probably aided that. The silence was killing me, so I asked General Aidan about the supposed gargoyle that turned herself in.

"Sure," he started. "She says her name's Ravine. She had a lot to say about you, actually,"

"Really passive aggressive, that one." Woodlaine added.

Aidan continued. "She won't talk about why she's even here unless it's to you. And we tried to get her to talk." He seemed annoyed at this.

"Yeah!" Packer blurted out. "She's a tough nut! All she's keen on is talkin' to you."

"I wonder why," I said, rolling my eyes. I hoped that Ravine would give me the answers to my 'Why'. I wasn't sure if she wanted something out of me, though. No gargoyle has ever tried to help our side before, and vice versa. I knew I'd have to be careful with what I let her in on.

King Klaus' speech filled in the silence that followed afterwards. "He served under me for over thirty years, always was humble and kind. With every pin added to his sash, he touched more hearts."

Commander Manning interrupted. "Well, for now, she's locked up. Her wings have been folded, and she's cuffed at all times."

"What did she do?" I asked.

"Nothin yet, but we can't take our chances. It's not everyday a gargoyle comes around offerin' info."

An abrupt applaud alarmed through the area, and King Klaus creaked his way down the steps. General Aidan's face hardly shifted, but his eyes were filled with dread. He breathed a long sigh walking past King Klaus, who patted his back. This was the speech I wanted to listen to. After King Klaus and the Commanders started talking and Aidan was up the steps, I walked to the wall under the stage. I didn't have to crouch as the stage stood above my head. I stood on my toes to see the closed casket on the stage. It sat on a table covered with flowers, small trinkets, and candles. Every flower was white, though different kinds, they were all white. General Aidan cleared his voice, causing the microphone's sensitivity to ring out.

"I worked under General Nutcracker for fifteen years before he retired. I will never forget the day he did, though. I was angry. I told him, I said, 'General, why would you leave us in a time like this? Why would you do that to us?'. And he told me 'I'm not leaving you, Aidan. I'm not leaving the people. I'm offering the position to someone much more able than I am: you' That made me so much angrier. I believed he was a coward at that moment- that he was too scared to fight anymore. But it wasn't because he was scared of what could happen, it was because he had hope for what could. He had hope for every single soldier he led. He gave us everything he had, and now it's time that we give everything back to him. For everything he accomplished, I will lead our forces to give it back tenfold. He was a role model, he was reliable, he was strong, he was everything we needed. He lives on in our hearts and swords as a legend."

I stopped listening when I peeked over the stage again to see Charles looking at me with a red face. None of his hair was tucked under a cap, even though he wore the rest of his uniform. His once tan nose had turned reddish-pink and his long eyelashes were wet with tears. Pitifully, I gave him a small wave. He waved back at me and I dropped back under the stage. I spent the rest of Aidan's time remembering what to say. With my back leaning against the stage, I got lost in thought trying to imagine what my cards said. Eventually, my train of thought led to Ravine. I wondered if she was the gargoyle I saw just before everything happened. It would make sense, but at the same time, it didn't. If she wanted to talk to be so bad, why didn't she just do so on the battlefield? I knew I had to be missing some piece of the puzzle.

I took a few deep breaths as General Aidan began to wrap up his speech. Just before he left the stage, he walked to the casket. I could tell that he was fighting to not let a tear roll down his face. He pulled something small out of his pocket and fiddled with it for a few moments, watching it reflect the sunlight at different angles. When he was finished admiring it, he carefully put it on top of the casket, in a nest of flowers. Aidan stepped hurriedly off the stage, and I hastily adjusted myself to face him. Without saying a word, he patted my back with a bit more aggression than King Klaus had given him. He seemed to be in a rush to get behind the stage. It was too many seconds later when I remembered that I had to go up there. Commander Woodlaine walked up from behind me and ran their fingers into my hair and rubbed my head, messing up the hair I had fixed an hour and a half ago. In a poor attempt to fix my hair again, I used my fingers to brush it back into place. Woodlaine told me that everything will be alright, which I was sick of hearing at this point, but I thanked them anyway. I bounced up the steps, and the sun poured onto my face. I squinted to shield my eyes and my heart dropped in amazement. The entire plaza was overflowing with people. Everyone stood shoulder to shoulder like a jelly-bean jar that was packed so tight the glass might break.

Every single one of those people was here for my dad. I couldn't help but laugh in amazement. I reached the stand, and in some spectacular miracle I almost forgot what to say.

"Wow. I could never have imagined this many people being here.

Thank you all, so so much for being here. From the bottom of my heart, this means everything." I paused for a moment to see if I could spot my team, and I could only spot them in the unfathomable crowd due to them being the only ones jumping up and down, trying to grab my attention.

"Before I start, I want to recognize everyone in the crowd who has served or is currently serving, so if you're a veteran out there or wearing your uniform tonight, I want you to raise your hand so we can give you a round of applause." Hands rose, and for what felt like forever people clapped. Finally it died down enough for people to hear me.

"Lately everyone's heard about what my father achieved as a soldier. People know it like the back of their hands. And it's definitely a lot to live up to, but I don't want him to just be remembered as a war hero. He volunteered at food banks, he helped build shelters for the homeless, he donated to so many different organizations. He was always ready to drop everything to help someone in need. It doesn't matter who they were, what kingdom they were from, or what the task was. I remember one day when he carried a pregnant woman and her groceries back to her house at the same time." I laughed at the memory, and so did the crowd.

"I feel so incredibly blessed to have been raised by him. Not because he was famous, or because he was cool, or even because I got to be a spoiled rich kid." I laughed at myself. It was weird to admit, but it was true. The audience responded with laughter, too. "It's because he taught me to be caring, welcoming, and he taught me to see that helping people was a good thing, not something that just took away from my time, and not something to do to get praised for. Not only was my dad able to climb to the top, he took everyone else with him. He inspired me, and so many other people to be their best." I turned around and looked at the casket, as if waiting for his approval, his encouraging smile.

"He may not be here with us anymore, but his hope and his encouragement still is." I paused, looking out into the crowd. I saw my team, I saw veterans and mountains of signs similar to the ones that still sit on my couch. I thought about what my cards said. But, on impulse, there was something else I felt was imperative to say.

"I promise everyone that I will live up to my name, and fulfill his dream." I saluted. To myself, to my dad, to anyone and everyone who could see. And that was a lot of people.

"My name is Nedrall Nutcracker. Remember me."

Six

A Series Of Horrible Decisions

I woke up in my cabin bed on a Monday for the first time in a week. After my speech, Everyone seemed to change the way they looked at me. When they saw me, they didn't think about what had happened that day, but they pondered what I would do next. That's exactly how I wanted them to look at me. Even General Aidan seemed to show more respect to me. The only one who hadn't changed even the smallest bit was Charles- to him I was just his best friend. He always saw me for who I was.

Today would be the day that I talked to Ravine. I tried to relax- I told myself it was just like another interview. But I couldn't keep my mind from racing. Every possible scenario blared in my head over and over.

With my uniform on, I walked with purpose to the dining hall. Dante was already ahead of me. Somehow, I spotted Paris first, and decided to follow her to the table. When I sat down, they were talking about their agenda for that day.

"I'm supposed to be helping create a more effective wing clip. General Codagh says the ones we have now are about as useful as a paperclip on an eagle." Paris answered.

"I thought they worked fine?" Charles questioned.

"They used to, but I guess we need better ones. Codagh says that General Aidan brought in a gargoyle and that we could test it on her."

"Apparently that gargoyle has somethin' to say to me." I spoke up. "So I've gotta talk to her today."

"And she just wants to talk? Strange." Charles added.

Fayola signed to me, asking if she had a name.

"Her name is Ravine. General Aidan told me that she says she turned herself in and wants to help us."

"Why would she do that?" Dante's brows furrowed in confusion, his mouth was full, but his confusion seemed to be stronger than his sense of manners.

"Yeah, that doesn't make any sense." Paris thought out loud, poking at her food with her fork. "Why would she betray her kingdom and people to help us win?"

"Yeah, what would be in it for her?" Charles mused doubtfully, poking his fork at his breakfast.

Fayola suggested that maybe the gargoyles had done something to her that made her want to switch sides.

"Let us know when you find out, I guess." Dante told me.

"I will." I replied as I set my fork down on my tray.

"Hey Ned," Paris stated, "We're going to the same place, let's walk together."

"Alright, let's go."

"Let us know how it goes!" Charles said, much too casually for the importance of the occasion.

We got up and started to leave. The smell of breakfast food and morning dew rushed to our noses as we stepped outside to cut through the courtyard sidewalk. I suggested we take a shortcut so we didn't have to go down the painfully long hallway Carol and I went through.

Which reminded me: "What's Carol been doing? Where has she been?"

Paris looked at me with a smirk. "Wouldn't you like to know," She giggled.

"What's that supposed to mean?" I laughed back.

"Pretty much everyone knows you've got a thing for her, Ned. At least the team does."

"What? I mean I-" She cut me off.

"We think she's into you as well, so don't worry, it'll play out well." Paris winked up at me. "She's been with the Generals a bunch, talking about how to protect her and maybe use her magic to help in the war."

"I've only actually seen her use her magic once. The memory is fuzzy, though. But I think she could hold her own." I replied.

"Really? What's her magic like?"

"It's kind of like a green and orange fireball. Like she could use it to light a fire or put it through someone's chest."

"Do you think she would?" Paris stopped.

"What?" I questioned her.

"Do you think she *would* do that to someone?"

"Well, She's done it before."

"What? Really?" Paris uncrossed her arms in curiosity. "When?"
"I found her once when we were kids- an ambush happened that day and we were in the woods. A gargoyle attacked me- a kid one- and Carol put a fireball through her wing. The fireball also happened to eliminate half my hearing, so I have the scar to prove it." I answered her, gesturing towards the flat side of my head.

"Wow," Paris said. "I didn't know you'd met her before. What happened after that?"

"Well," I tried to remember the details, but the last thing I'd ever been able to remember about that night was getting hit, then passing out in the snow. "I don't remember. The fireball knocked me out and I think Carol ran away. Now I know why, I guess."

"Wow," Paris' jaw dropped. "That's some crazy kind of power if it can just immediately melt a gargoyle's wing."

"Tell me about it," I laughed.

Paris laughed with me for a moment, then it was silent again.

"Do you know Ravine?" She asked.

"What? No, I've never met her." I refuted, more defensively than I had meant it to be.

"I just figured you knew her since she's so eager to talk to you."

"I don't have the slightest clue what she wants from me, and frankly, I'm kinda worried about it. What if she knows something about my dad? I haven't stopped thinking about it since he died, and now that this Ravine chick is in the equation, I'm worried she had something to do with it. I'm worried that I saw her on the battlefield the day my dad died."

I immediately regretted opening my mouth when I saw Paris' uncomfortable expression. "Sorry" Was all I could muster after that.

"No, I would be anxious too. Don't work yourself up about this gargoyle. That's probably what she wants anyways." Paris reassured me.

"Thanks."

We reached the building where Ravine was being held.

"Wish me luck."

Paris waved goodbye and wished me luck as I opened the door. The large metal handle creaked as I pushed it down, and the door slowly dragged itself inside. General Crixus-Wells, the General of the Drummer Boys, and General Aidan stood waiting for me inside. They were talking about something I couldn't hear, but they stopped when the door obnoxiously opened. Aidan stood straight, parallel with the wall, his muscles pushed against his clothes when he crossed his arms. Crixus-Wells stood with a wide stance, holding his head up high, arms crossed.

"Morning, General Aidan, General Crixus-Wells," I stood in a salute.

"Morning, Cadet Nutcracker. Ready for this?" General Crixus-Wells said, nodding his head to me.

"Yes sir," I said, waiting for General Aidan to let me off salute.

General Aidan saluted back to me, then we went back to standing normally. "She's in there now. Her hands are locked to the table and her feet are locked to the chairs, but Codagh hasn't come with wing locks yet. If she gets out of hand, we'll be waiting outside."

"Yes, sir." I nodded, and started towards the room that Aidan directed me towards.

This door was just as heavy as the first one I opened, but I tried to make it look easy since two Generals were right behind me. I turned the light on then shut the door behind me. I wondered if shutting the door was a mistake or not.

The girl that sat at the table wasn't what I had imagined, yet she was still eerily familiar. I did know her. She was the gargoyle that gave me that look, just before I found my dad on the battlefield. All of my worries and nightmares were starting to come true, but I couldn't let her or the Generals see that.

She had long black hair, and bangs that hung between two horns that rose up above her head, twisted around each other and then met at a point. I thought she might as well have one horn. Her face looked smoother than most gargoyles, who have scars and chips in their stone skin. Her eyes were such a dark purple that they might look black. She almost looked scared. Almost. I sat at the table and her hands tensed up in fists.

"Ravine? Right? What would be so specific that you insisted on telling me first?" I scooted the chair a little further back from the table.

"I felt like it would only be right for you to hear it first, straight from the horse's mouth." She answered, her fangs showing in white flashes.

"So?" Answers. All I needed were answers.

"First, I," She stuttered. "I want to tell you that I'm sorry. I'm sorry for your loss. That was never meant to happen. I swear. I want to help you."

"What do you mean it was never meant to happen?" I could feel the anger rise in my chest towards my neck.

"He was never meant to die," She said, louder the second time. "I would've stopped them-"

"Then why did he? Tell me why." So she did have something to do with his death.

"They killed the wrong Nutcracker."

"What?" My stomach dropped. "What are you talking about?" Dread, fear, and fury swirled in my gut. I put my hands in fists on the table to conceal their shaking.

"My plan the whole time was to betray my kingdom. I wanted to kill you so that your father would lay the final blow on us. They killed your father instead and I felt it my personal responsibility to tell you."

I couldn't respond; how could I? These weren't the answers I wanted, but they all made sense. My lips pressed together as I brought my hand to my mouth.

"If you hadn't killed them on the scene, I would have killed them myself."

"You looked at me that way, not because you knew what was coming," I paused. "but because you thought you did."

Just as I was starting to heal.

"And when we were children," She interrupted my thoughts. "I was at the ambush. I remembered you. They made my life hell for not killing you and the spirit."

"I don't care!" I boomed. "Why should I care what you've gone through? Why should I care what your mistakes cost you when they cost me everything!? Do you have some righteous vendetta against me since you couldn't beat me when we were kids!?"

"No, I promise this had nothing to do with you and the spirit beating me when we were kids! It was a horrible mistake!" Ravine bellowed.

"A mistake that cost the life of my father! A mistake that cost the life of a hero who hasn't had anything to do with the war for years! And all for what, your own vengeance against your own people?" I glared at Ravine as I yelled.

"Nedrall, please, I'm going to help you finish this war! They're after the spirit's magic. They're going to use it to imperialize everything." I could hear the desperateness in her voice- her despair echoed in her cries.

"I know that. Carol knows that." I finally looked up, and I noticed the way she was looking at me. She looked sorry for me, she looked embarrassed of herself. She looked like she might cry. I looked enraged beyond reason. I *was* enraged.

"Do with me what you will. But I am loyal to your King." She declared, composing herself.

"What did the gargoyles do to you?" I pushed my anger down. I wanted information about her, and beating her to a pulp in rage wouldn't fix anything.

"They took me from my family. I've been locked behind bars ever since that day. Public shaming. Public beatings. They use me and others like me as an example of what happens to gargoyles who aren't one hundred percent loyal to King Khelbent." She hung her head and looked at the table, her eyes lifeless.

"How did you escape?" I questioned. I needed to ask more questions to put her on the spot- I can't just trust the sob story of some gargoyle-especially not the gargoyle that got my father killed.

"I fought them. The guards. I escaped during the night. I flew from there directly to the attack here. I offered a squad of gargoyles a large pay to kill you and threatened to kill them if they failed to do so. They instead killed your father. I smirked at you because I'd seen the squad close by and assumed you were done for. I then flew away. I heard your screams and flew over to what I thought would be your dead body. I instead found you with your father and Carol standing behind you."

"How did you know that the fight was happening if you were locked up?" I interrogated.

"The guards were talking about it for days before. Everyone was talking about it." She refuted quickly.

"You say you left the prison in the middle of the night. The fight was during the daytime. That's a lot of time that's unaccounted for." I rested my elbows on the table and folded my hands.

"That flight takes a long time. The prison is secluded, and I flew alone without a map." Ravine looked up from the table.

I glared at her, taking her story into account. It seemed legitimate, but also all of it could be completely fabricated. For all I knew, she could just be distracting us from a raid and everyone could be dead outside the door. But I just had one more question without an answer.

"Why were you there that night? In the woods, when we were kids? Why were you out there as a child?"

"I could ask you the same thing." She dodged the question.

"I'm asking the questions here." I leaned forward, putting my elbows on the table.

She sighed and looked up at the ceiling. "I'm the youngest heir to the house of Khelbent."

"You're the king's daughter yet he's locked you in jail since you were a child?" I inquired. I knew he had four sons, but I never knew he had daughter. Now I knew why.

"No one ever said he's a good father. To be honest, I have it easy. You wouldn't believe what he puts my brothers through."

I largely wanted to avoid the depth of her family issues this interrogation.

"No one followed you here, right? Or saw you leave?" I changed the subject to something that probably should have crossed my mind ages ago. But she's been here for a few days, so surely if an attack were to follow her then it would have happened by now, right?

"That I can't be sure of. They should know by now that I'm not there, at the very least. But I don't know if they know I'm here. I didn't tell anyone, but I can't be one hundred percent sure no one saw me." She informed me.

"Are you serious? If someone saw you leave you could get us all killed." I snapped.

"We don't know that anyone did see me. And you can't blame me for the stealth skills lost in the time I spent imprisoned." Ravine defended.

"I sure as hell can. What are you here to do for us, anyways? Or did you just come here to give me your sob story and apologize?"

"Strategy and knowledge," She answered. "I could give you a route for an ocean voyage, leading directly into a trading port outside of the capitol. The port is largely abandoned, so no citizens for miles, and the castle is so close to it that you can see it from the docs."

"... Alright." I *hated* to admit it, but that was a great plan. Their kingdom didn't have any ports on our maps. I halfway wanted to kill her for what she did, but I couldn't. Now she wasn't just some captive- she was the key to winning the war.

And I had to live with that.

Just then, General Aidan pushed open the door and held it open for General Codagh and Paris so they could carry in the wing clips. There were two clips and each one was as tall as my torso and only a little bit wider than my head. It was a miracle that Paris could lift the thing, it looked like it weighed as much as the door that Aidan was holding.

Ravine looked up at each clip and looked at them with familiarity as she spread her bat-like gray wings, then folded them halfway in. Paris' eyes widened and her lips formed a thin line as she approached Ravine. While Paris seemed flustered, Codagh looked intrigued. She examined Ravine's wings closely and attached the clip to her wings and Paris did the same. Ravine folded her wings the rest of the way in and rolled her head, stretching her neck.

"May we have a moment to speak with her, Aidan?" General Codagh told more than asked.

"Yes, that's fine," Aidan responded, knowing Codagh wouldn't take no for an answer. "I'll have a word with Nutcracker in the time being."

With that, I stood from the chair I was sitting in- Codagh soon replacing me- and headed outside with General Aidan.

"So," I started, not sure whether I wanted to tell him the whole truth. "She does have a plan that could turn this war for the better."

"'Kay, what is it? She say?" General Crixus-Wells asked.

"She did. She says she can get us to a trading port of theirs that has no citizens around and it's within eyeshot of the castle."

"What's the catch," General Aidan protested. "If it was that easy, we would've found that route by now."

"Yeah, there's a catch." I said, dropping my shoulders. The room suddenly became very hot. "She said the port is abandoned. It practically doesn't exist on any of our maps."

"So there's just been some magical entryway this whole time and we just didn't know where it was?" Aidan asked, growing increasingly frustrated.

"How many ships do we have?" Crixus-Wells cocked his head towards Aidan.

"Enough." Aidan nodded.

I turned to the sound-proof and one-sided window that showed General Codagh and Paris talking to Ravine. Paris looked nervous- but not in a scared way. She looked like she didn't know what to do with her hands as she stood next to General Codagh. Ignoring Paris, I thought about what Ravine had told me about her failed assassination- if I was important enough to be considered assassinated. I wondered if I should tell General Aidan, and if I should tell him here, with General Crixus-Wells. Trailing off, my brain started creating the scenario in which I died instead of my dad. The world wouldn't lose much, but the people closest to me would. My father would have to bury his son, but Ravine was right- he would've had the drive to finish the war himself. Charles wouldn't be alone, he'd have the team. I'd grown close with the team, but surely they wouldn't be *that* moved if I died, right? Even if I did mean that much to them, my father meant more to more people, so his death has to outweigh mine by a million. General Aidan might care, but he's General Aidan, he'll get over it pretty quickly. And to Ravine's point- it might drive him to end the war more aggressively.

But, I didn't die. So now I have to fill the biggest pair of shoes in the world all because of Ravine's stupid, stupid mistake.. And it's all her fault. Deep down, I wanted to find some reason to forgive her. She didn't actively kill him, she told others to kill me and *they* messed up. And those people are dead now. She *is* trying to redeem herself, and admitted to all of it. If I told General Aidan, he might be able to help. On the other hand, he might just resent me for being alive in place of my father. I knew the mission ahead was the most ambitious one we'd ever faced. The Abbadon ocean was no joke- it was unclaimed territory between gargoyles and us. It's easy for them to cross if they fly, their endurance is so strong that they can fly for days on end. It only took them one night to reach us.

"Did she tell you anything else?" General Adian distracted me. He must have finished talking with General Crixus-Wells because he was gone.

"Um," I had to make a decision fast- do I tell him or not? "No sir."

Shit. I just lied to General Aidan- something practically impossible to get away with.

"Alright." He answered. Did I really just get away with that? "You and Paris will meet with me at 4:00 sharp in the east meeting room to discuss plans. I'll have a folder ready for you by then.

"Yes Sir." I saluted.

"Dismissed." Adian waved me off.

I walked back outside and into the courtyard. The enormous oak tree in the center provided shade over most of it, but speckles of sunlight still broke through the large layers of leaves. The weather was perfect- not cold enough to need a jacket but the light breeze allowed long sleeves to be comfortable.

I started to head back to my quarters in hopes to find Dante. I didn't know where the others were or what they were doing. But, when the ground started to slightly rumble, I knew I had to find them fast.

"Is it an earthquake?" I thought to myself. *"Where's Carol?"*

Before my mind or my feet could trail off, all three Generals blitzed into the courtyard with Ravine and Paris trailing behind them.

"What's going on?" General Aidan ran up to me immediately.

"I dunno, is it an earthquake?" I looked to the sky to see if the gargoyles had planned an attack. The skies were empty.

"I'm leaving Ravine with you two while we rally up the rest of the soldiers. Be ready to fight, and go find the rest of your team." Aidan instructed, while General Codagh unlocked Ravine's handcuffs and wing clips.

"What? Why?" I complained.

"I've given you orders, Cadet, follow them. If she wants to fight for us so bad then let her prove herself." Aidan ran off with the other Generals.

Ravine just stood there, awkwardly looking at Paris and I.

"What do we do?" Paris asked, trying to keep her balance as the ground started to shake even harder.

"We need to find the others." I replied, keeping my eyes on the sky.

"What do I do?" Ravine rubbed her wrists where the cuffs had held them down.

"Just follow us," I directed. "We're looking for a really tall girl with vitiligo, a short guy with orange-ish hair and another short guy with pink hair."

As Paris and I started to run around the base, with Ravine flying overhead, I pulled my walkie-talkie out of its satchel on my belt and spoke into it: "Addams where are you? Over."

Paris looked up at Ravine as we ran across the thundering ground. "General Aidan briefed everyone on your presence so no one should shoot at you, okay?"

"Yeah, I was thinking about that." Ravine replied, surveying the surroundings. Everyone was bustling back and forth to find their team, if they weren't all together already. "Hey! I think I see the tall chick you were talking about! Follow me!"

Ravine flew insanely fast, I didn't think I could keep up. But, luckily, Paris had no problem keeping up with Ravine, so I just had to not lose Paris and I'd be fine.

In no time, Fayola was in eyeshot and earshot. We yelled out to her, and she came running in our direction. She immediately signed to us, asking where Dante and Charles were.

"I don't know, I sent Charles a message on my walkie-talkie but he hasn't responded yet." We needed to get to our positions just in case this was going to turn into a fight with gargoyles, but we didn't even have our whole team. We were never going to find Dante and Charles in time. That is, if we looked on foot we wouldn't.

"Ravine and Paris, take to the sky and find Charles and Dante. Fay, we need to get to our positions now!" I pointed at Ravine and Paris.

"Got it." Paris agreed.

"Alright." Ravine grabbed Paris by the shoulders lightly with her talons and lifted her away into the air.

Fayola and I immediately took off to our positions, but as soon as we did, dead roots shot up from the ground one after another. One of them hit Fayola in the jaw on its way up, but she kept running anyhow. I unsheathed my sword and started slicing at the dead roots, and Fayola did the same. Bunches of thick, black roots broke through the dirt in a huge knot. As soon as they were out of the ground, the knots turned to ash and a gargoyle emerged from them. There were probably eight of them, but I was too shocked to remember.

Just then, Charles' voice came through on the walkie talkie. His words were hard to understand through the static and the walkie-talkie cutting on and off. "Yeah... we're just... already here... hurry up."

Fayola drew her bow and fired at the gargoyles one by one, and I charged them with my sword. The first gargoyle in my way had a spiked mace that was bigger than my head. I knew right away that that thing would crush my sword to pieces if I tried to block it, so I parried it swiftly and cut the gargoyle in the back of the knee with a spin. Immediately after that gargoyle was down another one jumped at me, its huge wings spread with fangs bared. I brought my sword down hard on its wing, completely detaching it from its body. Its momentum still lunged at me as it shrieked, so I swung my sword hard and fast to the right and cut open its abdomen.

Fayola had abandoned her bow and moved to dual sword fighting. She matched the gargoyles in height, but not in size. She was handling three gargoyles at once, but she was handling them easily, so I moved onto the three remaining gargoyles. I sprinted at them and swung my sword down at their chest heavily, only for my sword to be snapped by the gargoyle's wrist guard.

"*Shit.*" My mind quickly cycled through other things that might be attached to my belt. Nothing. I sighed and backed up, readying myself for a three-versus-one fistfight.

I examined the three gargoyle's builds. All of them were a foot taller than me, and two of them looked like a bodybuilder that could eat six cows for breakfast. The other one, though, was rather skinny. I regretted not having wrist and knuckle guards as I dodged the first gargoyle's punch and returned the punch to the skinny gargoyle's jaw. He reeled back but, almost immediately, the other two were back on me. The one on the right reached out to grab my shoulder, but I pushed his hand out of the way and pulled him by his arm behind me. I moved to where that gargoyle stood and turned to face them again.

"Is that all you two got?" I challenged in a false high of confidence.

"You're just a puny little toy soldier!" The gargoyle that I hadn't pulled away hissed, charging at me. Both of the others followed behind him.

I took a deep breath and clenched my jaw- I knew this was about to hurt. I punched the gargoyle that mocked me square in the face, effectively breaking his nose and my middle finger. I groaned in pain as he hit the floor. The skinny gargoyle tackled me to the ground from behind.

I kneed him in the gut, but to no avail. The gargoyle pulled out a dagger and laughed maniacally as it reeled back to stab me.

I gasped and held my breath as it smashed down its arm. I brought my arms up to block his arm, the edge of the blade just inches away from my eye. Without much struggle, I pushed away his arm and grabbed his wrist. I rolled the both of us over and took his knife from his hand, stabbing him in the chest with it. But again, before I knew it, the last gargoyle stood before me, holding his mace. With a deep, guttural laugh, he started to bring the mace down towards my head.

But then he dropped the mace, falling to a heap on the ground. Fayola stood a few feet behind him, still standing with her bow up and ready. She lowered it and smiled at me.

"Thanks," I laughed in relief. There was no way I was going to be able to dodge or block that mace with that tiny little dagger. "Let's go to the others."

Fayola nodded, and tossed me her sword.

We took off around the last corner of the base, to find that all hell had broken loose. The open field behind the base was burning with purple flames and bodies of both sides lay scattered in the grass. I found Charles and Dante amongst the crowd and sprinted towards them.

As we ran towards them, Charles was tackled by a gargoyle, who had him pinned down with her wings. She drew back a dagger of her own, and I knew there wasn't time for me to draw my sword to save him. Instead, I dove at the gargoyle and tackled her, pushing her off of Charles. I tried to avoid seeing my mangled middle finger as I stabbed the gargoyle in the chest.

Charles sat up with a huff, his hair tangled and knotted with grass and ash. "Took you long enough!"

I ignored his sass. "They must've followed Ravine here." I explained.

Dante threw a gargoyle over my head, sending him crashing into the dirt. "Are you kidding me?"

"She said when she talked to me that she couldn't be sure whether or not she was seen. It's all so stupid." I smacked the ground with my hand and stood back up to fight. "Where the hell are the rest of our soldiers?"

"I dunno! The Generals aren't here either! These stupid gargoyles have just been popping up out of the ground in their gross-ass roots!" Charles stood up as well.

Just then, the ground began to rumble again. The long, green grass trembled ever so slightly as small rocks and pebbles jumped up and down as the ground thundered. Everyone, even the gargoyles, looked around expectantly. Before I could turn around, a hundred deafening whistles rained down from the sky- each arrow piercing whatever had the misfortune of standing in its path.

Distantly, I heard General Aidan vociferate a command in a deep yell. I protected my head from the incoming arrows, but one pierced my back, just under my right shoulder blade. Suddenly, our own soldiers rushed the field. I finally turned around to see all the generals and commanders leading the rest of our military into the field on horseback. The leaders split up, and Aidan rode towards where my team and I were standing.

A shadow zipped overhead, and I whipped around, assuming it was a gargoyle in the motion of pouncing on me. It was a gargoyle, but not one that would attack me. Well, not anymore. It was Ravine swooping down to drop off Paris, before returning to the air to drop glass ornament-bombs on other gargoyles. Just as Paris landed, General Aidan reached us. But there was someone else on my roster that was missing.

"Where's Carol?" Was the first thing that came out of my mouth. I couldn't place my finger on why I got so nervous about the answer. I chalked it up to her overwhelming importance to the war.

"She's here somewhere," Aidan replied, examining the field all over, his eyebrows furrowed. "You can't miss her, glowing 'n magic 'n all."

"Yeah," I agreed with him, he was right after all. But I couldn't focus on the fight in front of me as my eyes darted around, desperately searching for that familiar glow.

Aidan dropped from his horse and unsheathed his sword in one swift motion. The gargoyles must have known who he was, as they scrambled to fight him. Aidan lowered his stance, silently observing his opponents in the few seconds he could. They pounced on him nearly five at a time, yet he swatted them away with ease. His sword moved continuously in one fluid motion.

I focused back on the battle happening before me. I tossed my sword to my left hand and balled my right hand in a fist, trying to keep my broken finger from moving as much as possible. A gargoyle landed in front of me, and I wasted no time swinging my sword at him. I was right-handed usually, but I probably wouldn't be able to hold it well when one of my fingers and most of my knuckles were broken in that hand. The gargoyle also had a sword, making the fight feel more like a fencing match as I moved my right hand behind my back. The gargoyle stepped backwards with every strike I blew. He looked worried but focused for the majority of the fight; I saw how his eyes tracked my sword with pinpoint precision.

Just as I knocked the gargoyle's sword out of his hand, I felt two Talons shove their claws into my back. I was shoved under the tall grass, sword still in hand. Before I could stand up again, I was being pulled into the sky by the gargoyle. They hauled me up at what felt like lightning speed, the wind created by their wings sent grass flowing almost flat in the opposite direction of them.

All the people on the ground started to become smaller and smaller before I remembered the piece of advice I was given the last time this happened: slice their ankles.

Still gripping my sword, I swung it behind my and sawed open the achilles heel of the gargoyle. What I didn't account for was my plan after I sliced them. I began falling exponentially faster towards the ground, and the gargoyle that dropped me shot back down at me. They screeched in pain as they threw knives down at me. I twisted in the air, narrowly avoiding the knives. Only one of them grazed the side of my shoulder. I forced my head up to look at the gargoyle, but before I could start it was already on me. They gripped my torso with their talons and strangled me with their claws. I yelled out as their talons sunk into my uniform, but didn't lose focus. I couldn't afford that yet. I pushed my sword through their abdomen as we hurled towards the ground. I decided that if I was going down, it was going down with me. With one swift slice of my sword, the gargoyle's wings fell off their back and away from the both of us. From there, it was a battle of who was going to break who's fall. I grabbed them by the shoulders and tried to force them under me, but neither of us could stop the momentum of us spinning. I tried to pull their claws out of my shoulders as we plummeted towards the ground, and I braced for impact. I squeezed my eyes shut and hoped for the best.

I noticed that the wind stopped blistering my face. I opened my eyes, and I was suspended in mid-air by oddly shaped tree trunks that continued to grow around me. They weren't the dead, black roots that the gargoyles created- it looked more like oak wood. Eventually, I noticed that everyone else that wasn't a gargoyle was suspended in these mysterious trees too. It was hard to see through the branches, but I saw the blades of grass tremble as the ground shook. At first, I thought it was the sound of the gargoyle that attacked me hitting the ground. But the screams of other gargoyles filling the air convinced me otherwise.

Between the cracks of the branches, I could see gargoyles writhing on the ground. None of them ran away or even crawled. The more I looked, the quicker I found out that they were morphing into wooden statues of themselves from the ground up. They couldn't move because their talons were rooted into the ground. In a state of panic, I pushed my way through the branches to see better what exactly was going on.

I saw Carol, standing only a few yards away from me. She was making the ground shake with magic. She was glowing so bright that I could hardly look at her, but I stared in awe anyways. Other people looked on with fear spread through their faces like the branches of her protective trees spread around them. I knew I should be shocked, or even scared, but I could only describe what I felt as amazement. She saved all of us- myself included- and defeated an entire army of elite gargoyles just by landing on the ground.

I'd never seen anything more beautiful.

Seven

And They Were Roommates

I woke up in an infirmary bed. The room was empty, but I could hear people talking outside the door. The room was grossly white- I had to squint to be able to look at anything. Sorely, I sat up. I didn't have a shirt on, but the majority of my abdomen and chest was wrapped in bandages. I must've passed out at some point from blood loss. I started to prop myself up on my bed, but immediately regretted it when a sharp pain shot through my wrist. Right, my hand is broken, almost forgot. Pretty much everything above my waist hurt as I propped my-self up against the plastic white headboard. The bed creaked loudly as I adjusted the pillows between my back and the headboard.

The door scrapedgfdagfad open as my eyes finally adjusted to the light. It was Charles. He walked in, carrying a clean uniform and carrying a walkie-talkie, which I assumed was mine since his was still attached to his belt.

"Well good morning, princess," Charles sassed. "You woke up quick."

"How long has it been?" I croaked, my throat still bruised from the strangulation.

"It's just the next morning. What do you remember?" Charles sat in a chair to the right of my bed.

"I just remember seeing Carol turn all the gargoyles into trees.

What else happened?" I remembered watching Carol's magic shake the ground and mutilate the gargoyles.

"Well, when we all climbed out of the trees, you were basically a stumbling blood fountain, and then you passed out. I don't even know how you managed to get yourself out of the tree, to be honest." Charles laughed as he sat my walkie-talkie on my bedside table.

"Is Carol okay? Where is she now?" I blurted without much thought.

Charles snorted back a laugh. "You're pathetic."

"What are you talking about?" I cocked my head.

He pointed past me, to the left side of the room. When I looked, there was no wall, just a large blue curtain that acted as one.

My eyes grew wide as I turned back to Charles. I pointed back towards the curtain and whispered hoarsely: "Is she over there?!"

Charles had to cover his mouth to contain his laughter as he nodded yes. I looked back over to the curtain, listening. I could only assume she was asleep.

"Is she asleep?" I whispered again.

Charles finally stopped laughing at me and caught his breath. "Yeah, she's been knocked out since the fight too. I think she used too much energy or something, but I don't know how magic works." Charles shrugged.

"Dang." I breathed, looking back over at the curtain. "How's everyone else?"

Charels sighed. "Everyone on our team is fine, but there were quite a few casualties. They definitely sent their elite after Ravine."

I groaned and leaned my head back against the headboard. I'd almost forgotten about that. "Ugh, she pisses me off."

The heart monitor gave away my rising anger, and Charles took note. "We don't have to talk about her."

"Yes, please." I rolled my eyes at the thought of her.

"How are you feeling?" He asked, changing the subject.

I took a deep breath, assessing the question. "Sore and light headed, mostly. Not bad, all things considered." I actually really felt horrible.

The pain was more in my head than anything, I had a splitting headache and my mind was swimming around Ravine and Carol and the others.

"I'll turn the lights down." Charles offered, standing and turning on the bedside lamp before turning off the overhead light.

"Thanks." I despised feeling so useless. But at the same time, I felt that If I stood up, I'd topple back over.

"No prob. Hey, I've got a lot of work to do, so I'll come back later, alright?" Charles rested his hand on the door handle.

"Alright. See you later." I said, massaging my throat lightly.

"*And stay in bed.*" Charles pointed at me as he backed out of the room, menacingly keeping eye contact.

I threw up my hands in surrender. "Yeah yeah. I got it."

The silence was both comfortable and uncomfortable at the same time. My head wasn't pounding as hard, but the quietness was dreadful. And I wasn't *doing* anything. There was nothing *to* do. I was too antsy to go back to sleep. The only noise was the incessant ticking of the clock on the wall across from me. I wondered if I should wake Carol up. Was she really just asleep? I heard the heartbeat monitor rise with my anxiety. We really didn't know enough about magic to know how to help her. We didn't know when she would wake up or even if she was really just asleep.

This feeling didn't leave for hours. All I could do was sit there and do nothing. Just me, my thoughts, and the increasingly annoying sound of the clock. Every now and then, I looked back at the curtain, debating whether or not I should try and wake Carol up. Every time, I decided against it. At first, it was because I wanted to let her rest. But then it quickly grew into the fear that she wouldn't respond.

I started to wonder where the rest of the team was and what they were doing. I knew they were either standing guard in case of another attack, or they were doing damage control. The building itself was fine, it was built to withstand these attacks, but the ground was probably all tore up. The only thing I hated more than being bedridden was doing yard work, so at least it wasn't so bad. Fayola and Dante both lived out on farms in the country, I was sure they'd be fine doing yard work. But when I pictured Paris and Charles doing it I couldn't help but laugh to myself.

Almost as if on cue, there was a knock on my door. Before I could respond, it chirred open slowly. I heard light footsteps followed by heavy ones before Fayola, Paris, Charles, and Dante turned the corner.

"Hey!" I greeted, excited to finally have people in the room, even if being the only injured one was a little embarrassing.

"Ned!" Dante beamed, immediately throwing himself onto me for a hug.

"*Uhf-*" I huffed, laughing through the pain. He lifted off me pretty quick and Fayola cringed at his action.

"How ya feelin' big guy?" Paris asked, sitting in one of the chairs lined against the wall to my right.

"Pretty good, just sore." This time it was true- my headache was starting to go away and the cuts started to hurt less. "Still feels like I'm swallowing nails and sawdust, though."

Fayola signed to me, telling me that she brought tea and soup for me after Charles told her that I, and I quote, "Sounded like I tried to chew and eat glass and was still choking on it."

I laughed and rolled my eyes at Charles' remark and thanked Fayola for the food.

"So, whatcha been doin'?" Dante asked, sitting in the chair next to Paris; Fayola sat down on the other side of Dante.

"Literally nothing, It's killing me." I groaned. I picked up the thermos that had the tea and took a sip. It tasted really good, and it felt good too. I didn't know what to expect, as I was never really a tea drinker, but I was pleasantly surprised. "This is really good, Fay."

Fayola smiled and clapped her hands together quietly.

"Oh yeah, Fay's a great cook. Whenever she cooked at her house back home, everyone in town could smell it and she'd practically have a line at her door asking for a bite!" Dante exclaimed.

"Were you in that line?" I poked fun at him. His volume started to make my head hurt again, but I wasn't going to say anything. It wasn't that serious.

"I was always first in line, bro!" Dante laughed.

"What about you guys, what have you been doing?" I croaked.

"Yard work!" Paris whined. "We have to fix the stupid ground since it got all tore up!"

I laughed wheezily as I fixed my posture. "I knew it! I'm glad I'm not out there."

"It's not all bad." Dante shrugged. "We're just making the dirt compact again. Right now it's like walking through gravel and sand."

Fayola nodded in agreement as I sipped more tea.

"Has Carol woken up yet?" Paris asked.

"No, not yet." I replied, turning to the still, blue curtain.

"I'd still be asleep too if I put so much magic into the ground that I made a whole new forest." Dante looked up at the curtain.

"It's a forest now?" I turned back to the three.

Fayola signed, telling me that all those gargoyles are still rooted into the ground and that they couldn't pull them out. She told me that they'd grown in the middle of the night into a forest.

"Wait, they grew into actual trees in the span of one night?" I remembered seeing the gargoyle's talons rooting themselves into the ground as they tried to claw themselves out.

"Yeah, it was insane. Everyone woke up and they were just trees." Dante didn't look like he was looking at anything in particular, his eyes just stared out.

"Just trees? They don't look like wooden gargoyle statues anymore?" I asked.

"Yeah. Just trees." Paris stared as if she could see it right in front of her..

I joined them as well. I remembered seeing a field full of the statues. I remembered seeing our soldiers wrapped up in trees like a cocoon.

"Where's Ravine?" Ravine was a subject I'd largely rather avoid, but I couldn't think of anything else after hearing about the new gargoyle forest.

"She's back at base. No one besides the Generals have seen her since the battle." Paris answered.

"I bet General Aidan's pissed." I scoffed.

"Oh he is. He's *pissed* pissed." Dante regained eye contact with me and nodded excessively.

"Yeah," My eyes widened as I took another sip of tea. "You guys have fun with that."

Fayola and Paris rolled their eyes, as if they were jealous of my position in a hospital bed, safe from General Aidan's post-shitty-battle wrath.

"He's just waiting for Carol to wake up now." Paris looked at the curtain.

"I think everyone is." Dante added, folding his hands together.

I looked over at the blue curtain. It stood so still and plain that it was hard to believe that there was actually anything behind it.

"What's Charles doing?" I broke the silence.

"Still working." Paris responded as she crossed her arms.

"Still? What time is it?" I looked at the clock. It was nearly 10:00 pm, and he'd come to visit me early that morning. He'd probably started working around 5:30 that morning.

Fayola signed 'I think he's distracting himself.'

"From what?" I cocked my head in confusion, but it hurt my neck so I immediately brought it back upright.

'From your injuries and Carol's injuries,' She signed, 'And what we all witnessed yesterday.'

It's true, Dante, Charles, and Paris probably saw a lot more than Fay and I did. They were caught in the thick of it as soon as it started.

"Everything will be alright." I reassured them as best I could. "With Ravine and Carol, the war is sure to turn in our favor."

"You're right." Dante agreed, a smile spreading across his face. "With Carol's magic and Ravine being a spy, we're sure to win soon."

Fayola and Paris agreed.

Fayola signed: 'We should probably get back to base before General Aidan realizes we've been gone for so long.'

Dante groaned. "Ugh, I guess."

"Can't I just pretend I'm injured too and stay here?" Paris tried.

Fay immediately shot down her idea with a stern look and a shake of her head.

"Alright, fine." Paris crossed her arms in defeat.

"We'll be back tomorrow, Ned. If we haven't been worked to death." Dante half-joked.

I laughed at Dante's exaggeration. "Alright. See you guys tomorrow."

They followed each other out of the room as they bid their good-byes, and then it was quiet again. The light as well as the lamp was on, and the longer I sat trying to ignore my growing headache, the worse it hurt. With a sigh, I realized I'd have to stand up and turn the light off myself. It wasn't a far walk at all, and my legs weren't injured, but I had stayed in bed so long that I almost forgot that I could walk.

I tossed the blanket to the side and sat on the edge of the bed. I still had the pants and socks of my uniform on, but the top half and my boots were nowhere to be found. I took off the pulse oximeter and stood up, immediately feeling light headed. My body didn't feel weak, but my head made it hard to balance. I guided myself towards the light switch and flicked it off with my cast, leaving only the light from my lamp and the overhead light on the other side of the curtain. I figured Carol preferred to sleep in the dark, so I started making my way to-wards the curtain. When I got there, I hesitated in pushing the curtain to the side. I didn't know what was on the other side. I didn't know if she was hurt or not. I held my breath and pushed it anyway.

She was laying there peacefully on her bed, eyes closed, chest rising and falling with each quiet breath. As I started walking past her bed, I realized I forgot to breathe again as I began to fall over. I gasped and caught myself on the bar on the foot of her bed. As I regained my balance, I jerked my head up to see if I'd woken her up. I hadn't. I sighed and walked over to the lightswitch on her side, flicking it off carefully. Now the only light was my lamp and Carol herself, whose warm glow still illuminated the dark. I followed the light and carefully pushed myself back in bed. At that point, the clock read 11:30. Carol had been asleep for a day and a half.

I adjusted the pillows so that I could lay down and get some sleep.

I felt more exhausted than I normally was at this hour. I figured it was a combined effort of the headache, blood loss, and doing nothing all day. I turned my lamp off and laid down. I winced a few times at the sudden jerks of pain in my wounds as I tried to find a comfortable sleeping position.

I finally found a comfortable and mostly painless way to sleep and started to drift off, dreading another day of not being able to do anything. Just as I was starting to fall asleep, I heard a click. I blinked, not fully comprehending what I heard. Had someone turned on my lamp? I could see my lamp- it wasn't on- but there was a source of light glowing behind me. I rolled over uncomfortably to see what it was.

Carol's lamp was on.

Immediately, I sat up and opened my mouth to say something. Nothing came out. I didn't know what to say. There were a number of things I'd like to say.

I heard her bed rustle and squeak, and I heard her breathing. Now that I knew she was up, I figured it would be more weird not to say anything.

"Carol?" Her name finally rolled off the tip of my tongue.

"Is that you, Ned?" Carol's voice spoke softly. "Where are we?"

"We're in an infirmary. Do you feel okay?" I spoke above a whisper, but my bruised throat made it hard to tell the difference.

"I feel fine, but what happened? All I can remember is arriving at the battlefield and seeing you falling, and I was scared. That's all I remember." I could hear Carol pacing around on the other side of the curtain.

"I don't remember much either. One second, I'm falling, next I'm caught by your magic trees. You used your magic to save everyone and defeat the gargoyles."

"What?" Carol asked uneasily.

"You saved everyone." I could hear the unsteadiness in her voice and tried to focus on the positive.

Slowly, I saw a bright, shaking hand hold onto the end of the curtain. The curtain slid back, and revealed Carol, standing there in her uniform and crying silently.

My heart dropped. "What's wrong?"

"What did I do to them?" She covered her mouth and sobbed.

Instinctively, like second nature, I jumped out of bed in spite of the rush of dizziness and walked to her. I put my unbroken hand on her shoulder and tried to comfort her. I knew how she felt; I remembered the first time I killed a gargoyle. I was nineteen and on some outpost with my father- I was only there to learn- but there was an ambush, and I was ordered to defend the post, so I did. That was the day I learned the truth about the gargoyle soldiers. I panicked and cried when I killed him. I thought I'd killed another person with a life and a family. My father told me the truth about King Khelbent. All of his soldiers are puppets sculpted from stone. Real gargoyles are usually born as citizens, into families. He has to make soldiers because none of his people, and evidently not his family, are willing to fight for him.

"You didn't kill them, Carol." I lowered myself to her level "They're puppets, not people. They don't have lives or families or anything like that, I promise."

"How could you know that?" Carol asked shakily through sobs.

"It's what my father told me. No one on their side wants to fight for King Khelbent so he makes puppets." I reassured her. "You didn't kill anyone."

She lifted her face from her hands just enough so that she could see over them. "Are you sure?"

"I promise." I rubbed my thumb lightly over her shoulder, trying my best to be comforting.

Carol's tears slowed and her breathing calmed down. She looked me up and down, now that I was illuminated by her magic.

"What happened to you? Are you okay?" She moved her hands off her face slightly.

"Oh," It was only at that moment that I realized I didn't have a shirt on, but several bandages covering my torso and neck. "Yeah, I'm fine. That gargoyle got me pretty good but I'm okay."

"Your voice sounds horrible, what happened?" She repeated her question.

"While I was fighting, it scooped me up and was gonna drop me, but I was too far up by the time I sliced its ankles, so I started falling. It was still attacking me while I was falling, and sunk its talons into my torso and started strangling me, but y'know. Just another Tuesday." I tried to make light of the situation.

"Oh my gosh," Her hands hovered over the bandages on my torso. "That sounds so painful."

"It doesn't hurt that much anymore." I reassured her.

She paused for a moment. "How long has it been since the battle?"

"Uh," I checked the clock on the wall behind her. It read 12:33 am. "Technically, the battle was the day before yesterday, since it's half past midnight."

"I was asleep for that long?"

"Yeah. Probably just exhaustion."

"Yes. Most likely." Carol agreed. "What's happened since?"

"Well, General Adian's pretty pissed off at the whole situation. Everyone else is okay, by the way. They've basically been doing yard work all day." I recounted what I'd been told that day.

"Yard work?" She moved her glance from the side to meet my eyes.

"Yeah, because the ground's all torn up from the roots."

"My roots?"

"No, the gargoyles' roots tore it up first."

"Oh, okay." Carol looked back down. "You're not just saying that to make me feel better, right?"

I laughed a little bit at her voice- I'd never heard it so soft before. "No, Carol. I promise you haven't done anything wrong."

"Okay." Her shoulders loosened and her hands dropped to her side.

I covered my mouth as I yawned. I shouldn't have been so tired, I hadn't done anything that day. My eyelids grew heavy regardless.

"You should get some sleep." Carol noticed my drowsiness.

"Yeah, that's a good idea." I agreed with her, but I didn't want to walk back over to my bed. I was more comfortable standing right in front of her. She was bright and warm, like a fireplace crackling on a cold winter's night. "But I don't really wanna move."

"Why?"

"Because you're so warm."

Carol laughed. "Well, you can be warm in your bed." She took hold of my shoulders lightly and spun me around to face my bed.

I laughed too as I made my way towards my bed, and she went back to hers. Before she got back in her bed, though, she pulled the curtain all the way back.

"What'cha do that for?" I asked, getting back into bed.

"So one of us will know if the other leaves." Carol explained.

I laughed a bit under my breath. "I'll know if you leave regardless."

"How's that?" She asked as she hopped back into her own bed.

"The room will be dark." I gestured toward her.

She snickered, looking down at her hands. "Well I have to know if you leave, it's only fair."

"I guess you're right." I agreed, hopping lightly into my bed as she did the same.

We both laid in bed for a while, neither of us being able to fall asleep. The ticking of the clock continued into the night, its noise periodically being broken by the rustling of sheets as Carol tried to find a comfortable position to sleep in. I didn't move much- there was only one comfortable way I could actually sleep in without agitating my wounds.

Eventually, I heard a loud sigh.

"Can't sleep?" I asked into the darkness, facing away from Carol's bed.

"No." She admitted, her tone filled with defeat.

"Why not?" I knew there were probably going to be multiple answers to that question.

"What comes next?" Carol asked, very matter-of-factly.

I thought about it for a moment. What comes next? Probably the plan that Ravine has. Probably a lot of other crap too. "I'm not a hundred percent sure. But we've got a solid plan now."

"What's the plan?"

"There's a port on the gargoyle's side that's abandoned. And it's right next to the castle. That's what the gargoyle told me, anyway. The Generals will make the final decision on what we do, though."

"What's her name?" Carol's voice carried softly through the air. I probably wouldn't have been able to hear her if my ear was to the pillow.

"The gargoyle?" Her curiosity confused me. I just told her that we had a practically foolproof plan to win the war and she wanted to know the gargoyle's name?

"Yeah! What's her name?"

"Ravine."

"Is she a real gargoyle? Or is she a puppet?"

"She's real. She's the princess."

"Strange," She said simply. I thought it was more strange that she had so many questions and so few at the same time.

"I guess." I sighed, trying not to move my torso too much as I breathed.

"And what about us?" She asked, nonchalantly.

That one caught me by surprise. I turned a little bit so that I could look over my shoulder. "What do you mean?"

"What will we do after the war is over?"

"Uhm, well," I didn't know who she meant by 'Us.' Did she mean her and I? Or the team? Or everyone? What am I thinking, of course she wasn't talking about just us. "I guess we'll do whatever we want. We probably won't have much to do during peacetime."

"I've never gotten to do whatever I wanted before." She sounded hopeful.

"What do you want to do?"

"A lot of things, I suppose. I want to go shopping and make friends and learn how to bake. I'd also like to fall in love."

Carefully, I rolled over to face Carol's bed. She was laying on her back, resting her head on her arms as she looked up at the ceiling. "Well, you've already done one of those things."

Carol moved her head to the side to look at me. "Which one?"

I wondered if she enjoyed confusing me with rhetorical questions. "You've made friends; you've got the team and myself."

"Yeah, you guys are my first friends." Carol's glow started to feel warmer.

"Really?" I inquired. I knew Carol was around my age- it was hard to believe she'd never made *any* friends before. "You've never had any friends before now?"

"Well, I've met kind people before. I've always had to live nomadically, so I could never stay around for long. If I stay in one spot for too long, the gargoyles eventually find me and attack the area I'm in."

"How long will you stay here?" I asked her. Tension rose in my chest as I realized that Carol might leave. Some burning feeling in my chest told me to never let that happen. It reminded me of the first time I ever saw her- she told me she couldn't stay and she had to go. At that time, I was powerless to keep her from leaving, but I didn't want to mess that up again.

"Well," Carol sighed dreamily and smiled. Her bright green eyes met mine; her gaze was soft. "I think this time is different."

"What do you mean?"

"This time is different, I think, because I know I'm safe here with you."

Again, I was sent back to the very first time we met. I jumped in front of her with a wooden toy sword and tried to protect her from a gargoyle. I didn't realize that that's what she remembered me as, not the kid who got knocked on his ass trying to look brave.

"I think I'm the one that should feel safe with you," I complimented. "You've saved my life twice now."

"We have saved each other, in a way." She started. "I have saved you from gargoyles, and you have saved me from gargoyles."

"When have I ever saved you from a gargoyle?" I laughed sarcastically.

"You protected me when we were kids, and after that first battle, I came back here with you. And now I'm safe."

"That's true, but I think that neither of those situations would have been different if I weren't there." I shrugged.

"But you *were* there." Carol emphasized. "I don't think that was a coincidence."

"So you think it was fate for us to meet?"

She paused for a minute, looking at the floor to think. "Well," She looked back up at me. "If fate is real, she's very cheeky." Carol laughed at her own words.

I laughed with her. "Fate or not, I'm glad we met."

"You are?"

"Yeah, I am. You're amazing."

"You're amazing, too."

We didn't speak for much longer after that, as sleep took priority in our minds. Even though I layed uncomfortable and injured on a stiff hospital bed, it was the soundest I'd ever slept.

Eight

Do Women Have, Like, A Hivemind Or Something?

When I woke up, Carol was gone. Her bed was neatly made and seemed like she'd picked up the rest of the room, too. Aside from exhaustion, Carol was largely uninjured, so I assumed she'd just gotten up to move around and find the others. I hadn't been awake for long when there was a knock on my door.

"Yeah?" I called out. "Who is it?"

Much to my surprise, General Aidan walked through the door with King Klaus. I remembered yesterday's conversation about how pissed off Aidan was after this whole ordeal. But, with King Klaus there, the tension was likely to be light.

King Klaus was the first to speak as General Aidan held the door for the King and I jerked myself upright, trying to look as presentable as possible.

"Good Morning, Cadet! How are you injuries healing?" He greeted me warmly, but loudly. His volume made me start to feel my heartbeat in my head, but I wasn't going to let them know that.

"I'm healing very quickly," I started, trying to sound as energetic as possible even though I'd hardly woken up yet. "I've been up and walking around, and I hardly feel any pain at all.

"That's good." Aidan said, letting the door close behind King Klaus. His face gave away that he didn't believe me. "You should be up and back to work in no time."

"Yes Sir." I agreed, the image of all the yardwork my team has been doing crossing my mind.

"Well," King Klaus set a tray of tea on the bedside table. "Since the battle took place, I've been serving my special tea out to wounded soldiers. So, drink as much as you need."

For a moment, I had forgotten that King Klaus was also a spirit. His healing tea recipe had saved many lives before. For a long time, it's what kept our Kingdom's territory in the war.

"Thank you, your majesty." I kept eye contact with the King, but seeing the tea in the corner of my eye made my mouth water. If I didn't have manners or any respect for the King and Aidan, I'd start chugging it right then. I just wanted to feel normal again so I could stop having to do nothing all the time. But, thankfully I do have manners.

"Of course, my boy," King Klaus chuckled. "Anything to get our wonderful soldiers back on their feet."

"And since I'm here," General Aidan started. "You might want to start drinking that, because Arenas are this afternoon. And you're fighting. We had it planned out before the attack happened, but since the attack *did* happen, we all agreed that it was best that you got healed up first."

"It was Aidan's suggestion to heal you first, actually." King Klaus looked at Aidan with a playful smirk.

I laughed- A bit awkwardly- but it was funny. It was hard to picture Aidan being outwardly worried about someone.

"Well, because you can't fight in the arena with broken ribs and a swollen neck." Aidan defended himself. King Klaus laughed to himself, and it took everything in me not to laugh with him.

"Fistfight or weapons?" I wanted to get as much information about the fight as I could, since Aidan already told me I was fighting and I was right there.

"Fists." Aidan answered.

"Who am I up against?"

"You'll see."

They bid their goodbyes, and King Klaus told me to drink up as they left the room. After they left, I noticed that there was an empty cup sitting next to the full one. I assumed it was meant for Carol, whenever she got back. I drank the tea, and I could feel the magic essence in it immediately bring the swelling in my throat down and soothe the pain in my chest. I knew the tea was magic, but I already felt like I was back to normal. My headache was gone, my throat didn't hurt, and it no longer felt like there were needles in my chest.

I stood up, putting on the clean uniform that Charles had left me, and grabbed my walkie-talkie. I used it to ask Charles where he was on my way out. As I walked down the halls, I saw other Cadets, who were also making a speedy recovery thanks to King Klaus' tea. It wasn't until I reached the doors of the medical unit that Charles responded to me. He let me know that he and the others were still in the mess hall eating breakfast. I told him I'd be there in no time.

It was uncanny how little pain I felt as I walked towards the base. The only pain I felt was a slight soreness in my chest and throat, but my headache was completely gone. Even as I walked into the noise of the mess hall, the room didn't start spinning nor did my head start throbbing. I found the table where my team sat, but I didn't find Carol there. I didn't have time to question it as I greeted the others and sat down.

"Geez, I didn't think you'd be up and running around so soon." Paris sat a half-eaten apple back down on her tray.

"The King's tea is no joke. That stuff worked in seconds." I replied, stealing a granola bar off of Charle's tray.

"Wow," Dante started with a mouth full of food. "I knew it existed but I've never seen it be used before."

Fayola perked up in agreement. 'I would love to have that recipe.'

"Isn't it, like, super secret though? I don't even think General Aidan knows how to make it." Charles asked between bites of his breakfast.

"Yeah, it's part of King Klaus' magic so only he knows the recipe. I don't think anyone else could make it even if they did know how." I answered.

"Magic's weird. Cool, but weird." Paris shrugged.

"So, you ready for Arenas then?" Dante rolled his shoulders.

"Yeah, I think so. I feel pretty good about it." I answered, realizing only then that I didn't know if I was going to be a better fighter than my opponent. The conclusion that this was either going to go horribly or wonderfully- nothing in between- settled itself in the core of my brain. "I just wish I knew who I was fighting."

"I might know!" Paris perked up, immediately grabbing our attention. "I overheard the generals talking about the fights. You're never gonna believe who you're up against."

I could feel the confidence drain out of me as I asked Paris who I'd be fistfighting. "Who?"

"Tyler Brown." Paris tried to contain her laughter. Dante and Charles did not.

"Oh. My. God. Are you serious? They did that on purpose!" Dante's laughter caused other Cadets to turn and look at us.

"Well," I started, trying to make it seem like I wasn't stressing myself out over this. "Now's a better time than ever to end whatever feud he thinks he's started."

I noticed that while the rest of us laughed over the irony, Fayola didn't look as amused.

"Oh c'mon, Fay, you gotta admit that it's kinda funny." I tried, wanting her to admit what she was thinking.

With a sigh, she signed to us that she hasn't seen Tyler or his team since the attack. Our laughter fell silent after that.

"I know we had some casualties," Charles started. "But his team is very capable, assholes or not. I'm sure they handled themselves fine."

Charles was right, they were more than capable of handling themselves. But then again, *I* almost died in that battle.

"You're right," I agreed. "Tyler might be a prick but he can hold his own. So can his team."

"Is Carol up yet?" Paris twirled her spoon between her fingers.

"Yeah, she woke up sometime last night, but she wasn't there when I woke up this morning." I answered.

"How's she doing?" Charles asked through a mouthful of food.

"She was a little confused when she woke up, but overall she's doing good." I figured Carol might not want the others to know about her crying when she woke up.

"Where did she go, though? It's not like she knows this place very well." Dante inquired.

Fayola signed to us that if she's not with the Generals, she's probably just exploring.

"Yeah, she's probably exploring. General Aidan's been busy handing out tea, and I don't think she knows where to find the other Generals except for Codagh. I don't know why she would go find Codagh anyways." I talked through the options of who she could be with, resting my chin in my hand.

Charles knew how to talk through my ramblings better than anyone. "So by process of elimination, she's just wandering around."

"She does like to wander." I agreed.

"I'll help you look for her!" Paris offered quickly, standing up from the circular cafeteria table.

Her sudden enthusiasm confused me, but I realized I should just go with it when Paris stepped lightly on my foot and gave me a 'Go with it' look.

"Okay," I stood up without retaliation and followed Paris. I didn't know what Paris and Charles were planning, or if Dante and Fayola were in on it, but I needed in.

When Paris and I got out of the Mess Hall, I started questioning her. "So why did you want to come with me to look for Carol so badly?"

"Because you, Ned, need to do something about your lil' Carol situation." Paris waved her hand in front of her, as if gesturing to something.

"My Carol situation? What are you talking about?" I looked at the space of air she was gesturing to.

"You need to ask her out already." Paris said, like we were playing a game of charades and I couldn't guess her clues in time.

"Ask her out? What makes you think she'd be interested in going on a date with me?" I reeled my head back in confusion. I didn't *think* Carol would like me like that. But a part of me hoped she did.

"Oh my God, are you blind? And deaf? And stupid? All three? You guys are head over heels for each other and Charles and I can't watch anymore." Paris groaned.

"Really?" I could feel my cheeks growing hotter. "You actually think she likes me that much?"

"See? This is what I'm talking about. You want her to like you. We're not in high school anymore, Ned. Take the woman out on a date like a man." Paris rolled her eyes.

"I mean, yeah, you're right. If you think It'll work, I'll try it." I only told her the tip of the iceberg. I wanted to gush about her, about how excited I was to learn that she might like me too. But, I feel like she noticed regardless.

"Okay, good. But first we need to find her. You said she was just wandering, right?" Paris nodded.

"Yeah. She's probably in the courtyard." I looked up, trying to remember how to get to the courtyard from where we stood. "You don't actually have to help me look, if you don't want to."

"Okay, but you better not wimp out on me." Paris pointed at me sternly.

I threw my hands up in surrender. "I won't, I won't. I'm going to ask her out as soon as I find her, promise." It felt ironic how much Paris cared about this.

"Okay, okay." Paris sighed. "Don't be late for arenas, though."

"I won't." I told her as we parted ways.

Truthfully, I had needed that push from Paris. I knew I had to find Carol before I started overthinking it too much.

Eventually, I found Carol standing under the tree out in the courtyard. Her hand was on it, glowing brighter than normal.

I walked up to her quickly, inhaling sharply before I waved and started talking. "Hey, Carol!"

Carol blinked back into reality before answering. "Hello, Ned."

"What are you doing?" I asked blankly, the important question sitting at the edge of my tongue.

"Healing this tree. It feels like it must have been here for a long time." Carol looked back at the tree.

"You can heal them?" I asked, following her gaze to her hand.

"Yes. It's why I used to spend so much time in the woods." She looked back at me with a smile.

As I stared into her soft gaze, I realized Paris was really right. I wanted Carol to stay in my life. "Are you doing anything today, Carol?"

"I suppose I'll be watching the arena fights today, why do you ask?" I could see her shoulders tense.

"Well," I started, taking a deep breath. "If you're not busy after, would you like to go out with me?"

A bashful smile crept across her face and she held her hands behind her back. "Of course I would! But, where would we go out to?"

I forgot that she might not be familiar with the idea of a date. "Well, you said you wanted to go shopping, right?"

"Yes! Let's go shopping!" Carol clapped her hands together and her small grin grew into a pearly white smile.

"Yeah! I'll meet you at the front steps of the base after the arenas?" I asked, my own smile mirroring hers.

Before either of us could say anything else, General Aidan spoke over the P.A. System, commanding us to "Move our asses to the arenas in five minutes or else we'll be working the horse stables."

Nine

Beating The Shit Out Of Bullies 101

After we sprinted to the arena, the team met up with Carol in the stands and I went to the entrance of the arena. I was picked- probably not randomly- for the first round. I would be fighting Tyler Brown. As I stood near the doorway to the arena, I examined the walls. Swords, spears, and weapons of the like were hung on the wall. They were dull, worn down, and scratched up. they hadn't been replaced in a while, even if they were meant to be dull in the first place. If not, people like Mack and Tyler would probably stab people like me with them.

Before I started stretching, I dropped my sheath and sash with my walkie talkie on the bench next to me. I recalled Dante and Tyler's fight as I straightened my legs and tried to touch my toes. I knew that Tyler was aggressive and impatient. He probably didn't take the time to examine his opponent, but then again I couldn't be sure. I stood up straight again and stretched my back and shoulders. He must have known that I was about the same size as him, so maybe his plan was to plow through me. He knew that I was a defensive fighter, and I know he's an offensive fighter. I thought about how I should go about the fight. I knew that he'd probably charge me, so I knew I could most likely just knock him off balance once he got close. In the middle of changing stretches, Dante snuck up behind me.

"Don't mean to interrupt, but I thought I would give you a heads up." He giggled at himself. "Haha, that rhymed."

I laughed with him. "No, you're good. I could use some info. I think I'm going to stay low and get him off balance. We're nearly the same size, so It'll be different than your fight with him."

"Yeah, he doesn't think when he initially charges, but when he gets close to you, he becomes really precise. He'll go for soft spots, like the throat and gut." He replied.

"So stay low, defensive, and don't give him an opening." I concluded.

"Yup. Nothing you can't beat."

I sighed and thought for a second. "I wish I was fighting Mack instead of him."

"Huh? Why?" Dante asked, moving to sit on the bench.

"I dunno, it's just," I adjusted my boots. "The way Mack beat up Paris the first time we were here. I wish I could do something about that, y'know? I don't really care about what Tyler thinks of me, but I wish I could put Mack in his place."

"Paris had a list of the people fighting today." Dante snickered. "Mack's egotistical ass wanted to fight General Aidan."

I stopped in the middle of getting ready and looked at Dante. "And what did General Aidan say?"

"He said he'd gladly do it."

I couldn't help but burst out laughing at Mack's utter ignorance. "Oh-h, he's gonna get messed *up*."

Just then, as if waiting for us to finish talking, General Aidan started talking on the loudspeaker. "First fight: Cadet Nedrall Nutcracker and Cadet Tyler Brown." The gate that blocked me from the arena rose slowly and I faced it, rolling my shoulders.

"Good luck!" Dante gave a playful salute before walking back through the entrance.

"Thanks." I said, stepping towards the field.

When we both stepped onto the field, cheers and screams echoed from the stands. The ground was dusty and the sun was hot as it glared at me from directly above, even though I could see clouds ready to roll in from a distance. I felt the adrenaline start to pump through me, and it felt good. I intended to hold true to what I told him before the last mission: I don't need my father to fight my battles for me. I've proven that time and time again, especially in the past few weeks. This battle would be the last 'I told you so', the last 'Look, I made it', the last 'My name is Nedrall Nutcracker. Remember me.'

I brought my head down from the clouds and lowered my stance. As expected, Tyler charged at me like a bullet. I waited. I watched him like a hawk and he did the same. In a matter of seconds, he was right in front of me, throwing a right hook. I dodged it and maneuvered away to face him again.

"Why'd ya move?" He huffed at me. Without an answer, I stood defensively, debating whether or not I should strike first. "You scared, Nutcracker?"

He stepped up to me, and swung another hard right hook. It was too fast to dodge. The crowd grew silent, holding their breath. I maintained my stance, though I had to step back as my body followed my head. I turned back to him, and he swung again with the other fist. This time, I blocked it. I used my forearm to quickly move his fist away from me, and before he could think I punched him with my left fist. While he recovered, he stepped backwards and I knew this would be my time to get him off his toes and onto his ass. I brought up my foot swiftly and side-kicked him in the gut. But just as soon as he hit the ground, he was back on his feet. I moved closer to him, arms ready to block his. It was taking too long for him to make a move, so I did. I charged him, and ducked to dodge his punch. I grabbed him by the shoulders and kneed him in the gut. I got a few more hits in before he pushed my knee down, and brought his leg to my side. I knew this was the preciseness Dante told me about, but before I could react, I had been knocked to the ground.

He came down like an elephant's foot on top of me. The brawl was an ugly struggle of punches and pushes. In an effort to move his hands off my shoulders, I brought my arms to my chest and quickly spread them out through his. I pushed him off of me with all the strength I could muster in the small timeframe I had. The people in the stands had begun yelling again. I wasted no time in getting on top of him and punching him in the eye. I aimed for the nose, but I'll take what I can get. With his eye half open, nose bleeding, and lip busted, I almost felt bad for him. Blood from my nose fell onto his face as I pushed his shoulders into the dirt with all of my might. The match was beginning to feel more like a real brawl than a spar.

He swung, and swung and swung. Each hit went to either my face or throat. Hardly budging, we both realized there were only a few seconds until I won. He growled and cussed with anger, but I kept pushing him down, knowing I was almost there. I heard the crowd chant behind me, counting to five. The force that Tyler and I were exerting grew with the numbers. When they hit five, I released my hold and rolled over onto my back. He sat up halfway facing the opposite direction. That head-ache was coming back- likely from the fresh black eye and busted nose and lip. Everyone was cheering, yelling, and I saw excitement in the crowd's faces.

I was confused when their faces quickly changed to express fear, so I looked over at Tyler, who was reeling his fist back for a punch. When he threw the punch, I dodged it only by a centimeter.

Pushing him away so that I could stand up, I yelled at him: "Dude, what the hell are you doing?"

"I hate that pretty boys like you get everything they need from the second they can hold a sword! All you are is daddy's boy, an exact copy of him!" At this point he was already on his feet, still bleeding pathetically. " You never worked for anything to get here!"

"What do you want me to do, apologize!?" I didn't know if the audience could hear me, but at the moment I didn't care. " I know that people like me get everything we need from the get-go and I'm not saying it's fair but I still worked damn hard just to be here! I have to prove myself just as much as everyone else, if not more."

"Yeah, now that daddy dearest can't give you the job himself." He barked, getting in my face.

"You shut the hell up. You're already going to be under suspension for fighting past the time limit, I'm sure you don't want a snapped spine to go with it." I snapped back, holding him back just enough that he couldn't push me but not so much that I was pushing him too.

He was about to open his mouth again and I was about to beat him, again, before General Aidan and all three commanders got between us. Commander Packer stepped between us and General Aidan slapped Tyler so hard I thought he might fall over. Before I could smirk at it Aidan turned around and told me that if I had hit him back I'd be slapped and on suspension too.

I told him that's the only reason I didn't do it.

Commander Woodlaine turned to me. "You alright kid?"

"I'm alright, Commander." I looked away from Aidan, who was verbally ripping Tyler a new one, to Commander Woodlaine.

"You're excused. Patch up your nose and get to the stands." They said, waving me off.

"Yes, Commander." I saluted and left, grabbing my things I left on the bench and wiped my face with a tissue from the recovery cabinet, which was just a box of tissues and a roll of bandages.

When I got back up to the stands, Carol and Dante were the first to greet me.

"Are you okay?" Carol asked me.

"What happened down there?" Dante followed up.

"I'm fine, my nose isn't bleeding anymore. I guess he got angry after I won and he started swinging at me again." I answered them.

Charles started talking. "What did he say? He looked pretty mad."

"Just another prick that's pissed about me being 'The Nutcracker's' son, that's all." I put hyperbolic emphasis on 'The Nutcracker' and shrugged.

Fayola signed to me, asking how I responded to him.

"I told him to watch his mouth. Honestly, if General Adian didn't show up when he did I might've gotten myself in trouble too." I looked down into the arena field to see the commanders leaving with Tyler and General Aidan standing in the arena, waiting. "I guess Mack's fighting next?"

"Yup!" Dante laughed so hard his face turned red. "This sure is gonna be a show."

"I hope he gets his ass beat." Paris said, crossing her arms.

"Oh he will," Dante responded, still laughing. "He doesn't even come close to General Aidan's skill."

Only a moment later, the gate opposite of Aidan opened and none other than Mack Kingsman stepped onto the arena grounds. Commander Woodlaine started to announce on the loudspeaker.

"Next Round: General Aidan Ambercroy and Cadet Mack Kingsman." The speaker cut off Commander Woodlaine's snickers.

I could see Aidan yelling something to Mack from across the arena, but I was too far away to hear. His face said everything I needed to know. If I knew General Aidan, he would humble Mack right here in front of everyone.

Before they approached each other, Charles grabbed my attention. "Let's get closer!" He said, and as I followed him the others fell behind. Soon enough we were in the very first stand, and Mack approached Aidan slowly.

Aidan hardly moved at all, never taking a step forward and only turning to face Mack, who was approaching him quickly but carefully. From here, we could hear their discourse.

"You can't back out now, Kingsman. If you were paying attention the first time, I told you guys that you only get one shot at this per individual, and not to embarrass yourself. I hope you're feelin' lucky." Aidan cautioned him, in a confident diction I'd never heard from him before.

"You talk a lot of smack, Sir, but you haven't made a move yet!" Mack yelled, finally reaching Aidan and standing dangerously close.

"Why should I make the first move," Aidan started, pulling Mack towards him by the arm and letting Mack trip over Aidan's foot before sending him straight into the dirt with a kick to the back. "If you're going to make it for me?" Light on his feet, Aidan turned back to him. Aidan could've pinned him and won right then, but I could tell he was getting a kick out of this.

Mack jumped angrily to his feet, running at Aidan. Mack threw his fist as hard as he could at Aidan's head, and was shocked stiff when Aidan caught it in his tracks. Aidan punched him in the gut, then when Mack heeled over in pain Aidan brutally drove his knee into Mack's chest. With grace, Aidan swept his leg through Mack's, knocking him onto his stomach.

The crowd flinched as if they could feel the pain themselves while Dante was laughing so hard I had to make sure he was still breathing. Paris, though, was watching with malicious intent. Fayola seemed like she was studying the fight and Carol almost looked scared. Charles re-assured her that he definitely deserved it. I went back to watching the fight, and Aidan had Mack pinned face first into the dirt. As hard as he tried, Mack was no match for General Aidan. It almost seemed unfair, but it was well deserved. I'm sure Paris would agree.

Commander Woodlaine took over the loudspeaker, and started counting. "One... two... three... four... five!"

Aidan let up, and Mack stood up.

"You better get over whatever's going on before your buddy gets back, if not you'll be out of here before you can fall on your ass again."

"Whatever." Mack huffed.

"What was that?"

"Yes sir."

Paris giggled to herself which led me to notice that Dante finally got down to a normal laughter level. Charles and I laughed with them.

"That was definitely worth the watch." Charles leaned against the short, concrete wall that barred us from the arena.

"For sure," Paris started. "He had that coming from a mile away."

"Yeah," I looked over my shoulder to see Mack leaving the arena. "He'll pull himself together." I turned back. "Tyler though, he's gonna have it rough until he learns to keep his mouth shut."

"Oh yeah, Brown's a jackass but at least he has the brawn to take on somebody like Ned, even if he is an idiot." Dante joked.

Fayola signed: 'Both Kingsman and Brown have the potential to be great soldiers, but they can't get the purpose of the job through their thick skulls.'

"You said it sister!" Charles and Fayola high fived, except it wasn't very 'high' for Fay.

"And what is it to you, Fay?" I crossed my arms in thought. "The purpose of the job, that is."

She signed back and told me that she believed the purpose of the job was to serve the throne and protect the people. Dante added that being good at the job might help them, too. If Carol hadn't spoken up then, I might've forgotten she was there.

"Why do they give you so much trouble for being General Navid's son?" she asked.

"Because they want what I had growing up." I replied, simply.

"Carol, honey, you're gonna learn that some people are just complete and utter dicks. You gotta learn to just let them be dicks by themselves." Charles added.

"As for Tyler, I think he just spites me personally." I said. "He's only ever seemed to have something to say to me- he fought Dante by chance."

"A lot of people always have a lot to say to you, Ned, that's how it's always been." Charles said.

Carol joined back in the conversation. "That makes sense. I mean, it doesn't, really, but I guess I understand their point of view."

"Anyways, we have a bunch of freetime after the arena fights today, you guys got plans?" Dante asked.

"No, I have plans, sorry." I responded, glancing at Carol who was trying to control her laughter with her hand on her mouth.

"What do you mean you have plans? Since when do you have plans outside of work and us, Ned?" Charles sassed.

"I guess you took the hint. Bout' time, player!" Paris lightly nudged me with her shoulder.

Carol could no longer contain her laughter and when it clicked, Dante and Charles gasped. Fayola looked like a proud mother.

"Yeah! It's about time, Ned!" Charles poked fun at me. "I've been waiting this whole time for you to ask her out."

"Yeah whatever, come back when you've got a boyfriend, Charles." I rebutted

"Boyfriend?" Dante asked.

"Dante, literally what about me says 'I want to attract women.' to you?" Charles posed for him, putting his hand on his hip.

"True." Dante agreed.

"It's just a first date, guys, don't get your head in the clouds." Carol blushed.

"Yeah, don't get your head in the clouds, Ned." Charles stepped on my foot.

I slid my foot out from under his and punched him in the arm playfully. "Whatever, dude."

General Aidan was back on the loudspeaker, and was counting the seconds for the next fight. He didn't even sound tired. But with that, the final match was over.

Ten

Walking in a Winter Wonderland

Before Carol and I split to clean up before our date, we decided on going to a park. I wanted to change out of my uniform now that both me and it were dirty and bloody, and Fayola and Paris insisted they wanted to help her get ready. On my way to my room I thought about the circumstances of our date. We originally met when I was years old, we met again recently after experiencing the passing of my father, and now the both of us have feelings for each other. We knew little to nothing about each other, but we'd already experienced so much together. We've supported and protected each other even though we're strangers. But I think that strengthened our relationship rather than weakened it.

Upon entering my room, only Asam and Basil were there. At this point I wondered if they even had a job to do, since they were always conveniently doing nothing.

"What's up?" I greeted, already pulling off my sash before I could close the door.

"Ah, nothin'," Asam answered, to no one's surprise. "Your fight out there was brutal, you best be glad he'll be gone for a hot minute."

"yeah, well, I have more important things to do than worry about what Tyler thinks about me."

"Like what?" Basil chimed in.

"A date." I picked up a white buttoned shirt and navy-blue trousers. The shirt had a little bit of frill at the end of the sleeves and around the collar, and I paired the outfit with white boots. I didn't want to dress up too much- Carol didn't seem like the type of woman to enjoy extravagance. After a moment or two of more banter I dressed myself and was off. I walked out to the main entrance of the base, and there was snow, falling onto the pavement like flower petals. It was too warm for them to stick, though. I hadn't waited for very long when she presented herself to me. If I thought she glowed before, now she was a star. She seemed to levitate in a light, sage green dress. It flowed elegantly down to her feet, the balloon sleeves softly surrounded her wrists up to her shoulders, where they connected to the torso piece with small bows. The top piece flowed in a V shape into a corset. Her elegant evergreen hair was down, flowing like a calm stream. I was stunned. I went to greet her, being pulled to her like a magnetic force.

"Ned! Oh, you look like a prince!" she clapped.

"You're beautiful." I blabbed. I knew that both my father and I had zero game. I could write a book of poems to describe her beauty to me but my mouth couldn't speak them.

Mesmerized, I took her hand and bowed, lightly kissing her fingers.

"Before we go to the park, I'd like to show you around town." I suggested.

"Let's go!" Carol said excitedly.

With her hand still in mine, I led her towards Main Street.

I remembered that she'd never seen a city before as we looked through all the shops. Bakeries that filled the streets with the scent of bread, bookshops that looked so comfortable that you could sink into their sofa and read for years. We went to a food market, where she ate seafood for the first time. Seafood is a rarity where we live, so I told her that when we travel to the sea we'd cook whatever she liked however she liked it.

I noticed, however, on our way to the park, we got looks and glances from people who had recognized me. No one came up to us, and as far as I was aware there were no pictures taken of us.

We arrived at the park and instantly, it was quieter than the streets of the city. Instead of bustling people and noisy roads there were running rivers and small gusts of wind, pushing snow onto the trail, just for it to melt away at contact with the heat of the stone path. Large oak tree leaves rustled every now and again and quite a few of them fell, which we both agreed was the start of the best season.

"Have things been going well for you at work?" She asked after a silent moment of thinking what to say next.

"Mostly well," I brushed off the topic of the circumstances of my father's death, and instead chose to talk about the plan for the following month. "With the new information we have and a gargoyle on our side, we can head to sea next month."

"So you all will attack the gargoyles?"

"Yeah. But we'll get there at a spot where there's no civilians, so no innocent lives get hurt." I answered.

"That is good." Carol nodded. "Do you think this will be the end of the war?"

"I hope so." I laughed. "I really hope so."

"So you're using this month to prepare." Carol started. "Did...did the gargoyle tell you anything else? Paris told me when she came to get me for the arena that you looked off when you left the room with her. She told me you looked angry."

Paris, you little snitch. So much for not saying anything. "Well, yeah, a little bit."

"What is it? You can tell me." Carol took my hand and looked up at me gently.

"The reason she came to us was out of guilt. She sent a troop of gargoyles to kill someone and they ended up killing the wrong person." I noticed her looking into my eyes. I tried not to let tears well up as I looked back into hers.

"No," Carol gasped. "You don't mean-"

"Yeah. But, I mean, there's nothing I can do about it now." I felt my voice begin to crack.

"Oh, Ned. I am so sorry." Carol pulled me into a tight hug. "The world has not treated you well at all lately. You don't deserve any of this."

I sank into her arms, it wasn't my plan to break down on our first date but she was right. Fate hates me lately. "I'm sorry, I..." I cried quietly. "I feel like such a baby- crying on a first date."

"Oh Ned," Carol held me closer and rubbed my back lightly. "I don't mind. You deserve to cry and be angry at the world."

"You're the best." I said through a mix of crying and laughing.

She let go of the hug and I wiped the stray tears off my face. She rubbed my face- her hands felt like the warm heat of a fireplace. She took hold of my hand and we continued walking.

"You fought very bravely today, Ned. The other one made a fool of himself for breaking the rules." Carol spoke.

"Thanks," I said, both for the compliment and for changing the subject. "That guy really didn't like me, so it made beating him that much harder." I stopped for a moment. "What about you? I don't really know that much about you."

She giggled at this. "Oh, what is there to know, really? I haven't got many hobbies, or friends. I was hidden away from the gargoyles for all my life. And now here I am, standing with you, feeling like the luckiest girl in the world."

"Well, you're a part of the team now, Carol." I wrapped my arm around her shoulders. "And you don't have to spend your life hiding from them anymore."

"I'm glad." she smiled. "I'm glad I get to spend the rest of my life with you guys. With the team."

"Me too."

The more I thought about it, the more I realized I liked everything about her. I also realized how much I actually did know about her. She likes the 'Fancy toast' at the bakery that has raspberry swirls in it, and velvety soft couches, and bookshelves that are bigger than her whole body that hold stories that are even bigger. She likes the smell of cooked salmon and poking fun at the way my boots click in on the ground. She likes me, too, I hope.

"So what do we do now?" She asked, stopping our walk next to a lake.

"You can use magic, right?" I requested eagerly.

"I can! Have you not seen it before?" She clasped her hands together buoyantly.

"I have before, when we first met. Y'know, when you shot that fireball at the Imp's wing?" I alluded to the scar that resides where my left ear used to be.

Her gasp turned into a giggle. "Oh my goodness! I had forgotten about that! It hasn't troubled you too much, has it?"

"Only a little. It's good enough for the workforce, it's good enough for me!" We laughed.

"Since the gargoyle was a child, her wings were not as sturdy and I think that's why they ripped." she added.

"You're probably right." I stepped onto a wooden dock that edged into the lake, and looked out over the water. Looking at my reflection, I noticed how the flat side of my head really looked. I hadn't paid it any attention in a while. Then, without warning, I was knocked off balance and splashed into the lake. I looked up and through the rippling water, I could see Carol's refracted figure laughing. When I popped to the surface, she bent down and got closer to me.

"Are you alright?" She said between laughs. "Here, let me help you." she reached her hand out to me.

The opportunity was too great to miss, so with a smirk I grabbed her hand and pulled her into the water. She grasped her nose and mouth as she fell, and she quickly arose, catching her breath and wiping her eyes.

"You!" She splashed water at me. "My dress is all wet!"

"So are all of my clothes!" I grinned.

She laughed with me and then ducked underwater. Looking through the dusty blue water, I saw her figure glow, and she seemed to propel to the center of the lake.

When she came back up, she yelled to me from the center: "Do you want to see my magic?"

"Yeah!" I called back.

she brought her hands underwater, and the surrounding water began to glow a brighter blue. Swiftly, she brought her hands up and the water with them. With force, she pushed her hands towards me and sent a wave after me. I would have swam away, but the wave cornered me into the dock. It didn't hit hard, but it did push me quite far under the water. I opened my eyes and saw the blinding light of the sun. When I turned, I saw something even brighter. Rays of green light whipped around underwater, surrounding me. They closed in on me, pulling me through the water and up out of it. When I reentered the air, I was suspended above it by what I can only assume to be Carol's magic, and before I knew it, I dropped back into the lake. The water was calm now, as if neither of us had moved an inch in it.

As I caught my breath I attempted to fling out the water that had filled my ear in the wave. Preoccupied with my ear and keeping myself afloat, I was temporarily deafened and was not paying attention to my surroundings. I titled my head sideways and held it, squinting to keep the sun out of my eyes. I could see that I was now near the center of the lake, so I started swimming towards the dock, only barely hearing the swishing of the water around me. I pulled myself up, and noticed Carol propelling herself toward me with a worried look, and I started to wonder if she called out and I couldn't hear.

She pulled herself onto the dock next to me, and started speaking rapidly; I couldn't read her lips, so gently I told her to hold for a minute. Finally, I could hear my surroundings.

"Sorry, what were you trying to say? Water got in my ear, I couldn't hear you." I told her, pointing to my ear.

"Is that what happened? Oh, Goodness, I thought I hurt you! I called out to you and you didn't respond, then started swimming and fiddling with your head."

"No, I'm fine, I promise. That was great, though! Your magic is really cool." I tried to reassure her.

"You think so?" She twisted her hair to wring out the water.

"For sure! It looks like the northern lights. What are those called again?"

"Aurora borealis." She responded.

"Right. Aurora borealis."

"I suppose it's time to head back now." She sighed. "You've probably got more planning to do."

"And you've got to get a uniform." I told her.

"I do?"

"You're a part of the team now, you've got to look the part." I stood, and she did as well.

"Where do I go for that?"

"Well first you have to get a dry dress." I laughed. "Then maybe go to Fayola or Paris for help."

"Alright." She nodded as we started to head back to the capitol building. I wrung out my shirt the best I could while wearing it, and hoped it would dry enough by the time we got back to base. While I did that, Carol was tying her hair back. She twisted her long ponytail around in a spiral until she could wrap the tie around once more to wrap her hair in a bun. She was practically dragging the heavy dress with each step, careful not to step on it and trip.

"How about we stop and get dry clothes first?" I offered.

"That sounds like a good idea." Carol agreed.

My next stop would be General Aidan's office, and I knew I could only go to General Aidan in my uniform, which was at base, but The least I could do was get Carol dry clothes. Even though she pushed me in first.

"Where do you usually go?" I asked, forgetting she's never been here before. "Nevermind, dumb question, I'll call Paris. Just have to find a phone-" I looked around after we exited the park gates, and saw a phone booth nearby. Carol laughed to herself and followed me to the booth. I put a few coins into the slot and called Paris. Soon, she answered.

"Hello?" She spoke.

"Hey Paris, where do you usually shop for clothes?" I asked.

"Um, I don't know, when I moved here I went to Capitol Avenue.

I'm not from around here, but if you're shopping for Carol then Capitol Avenue's your best bet. Also, you need to be heading back here soon so you can be ready for the meeting with General Aidan about Ravine."

"Right. Thank you, bye."

"You're doin' great, champ, buy her heart out." Paris joked.

I laughed. "Shut up, Paris."

"Alright." I turned to Carol. "Capitol Avenue."

We were off, walking with purpose when Carol said, "Makes sense, we are at the Capitol after all."

"Yeah, I know this place like the back of my hand. It's where I grew up." I said.

"You did?" Carol asked.

"Yeah, the forest near here is where I met you for the first time, during that ambush." I arrived at the end of Capitol avenue and stopped, Carol also pausing next to me.

"Right." she responded. "Where to?"

"Pick a store, any store" I waved my hand in front of us, gesturing to all of the clothing stores nearby.

After debating her options, Carol made her way to the closest store. We walked in silently, as the store was mostly empty. A small bell chimed as we opened the door and the place smelled of lavender. Racks of clothing hung on the walls, hiding the tan walls behind them. In front of the racks were tables with more clothes stacked on top of it. One man stood at the front desk, watching us carefully, but happily. The store was as clean as a tub. Not one speck of dust, strand of hair, or even a fly was to be found anywhere. Sooner than I thought, Carol was carrying much more than one dry outfit. But her expression was worth more than every article of clothing in this store. I rang it up and Carol went to the changing rooms. Meanwhile, the old man at the desk made small talk.

"You're Cadet Nutcracker, right? I read about you in the paper a few weeks ago."

"Yes sir, that's me." I responded.

"I served with your pops, y'know? I retired after the battle with the mouse king. I was his Commander. After I retired he brought up this kid named Aidan. You know Aidan, yeah?"

"Of course, sir. General Aidan took over my father's position when he retired. It's great to meet you, thank you for your service." We shook hands, and it reminded me of when my dad would make me practice handshakes with him. Firm, but not aggressive.

"Is that your little lady you're buyin' clothes for?" He asked, pointing to the dressing room.

"I don't think I can call her mine just yet." My eyes followed his gesture.

"Oh," He rolled his head and eyes like he didn't believe me. " I know you're a good kid, and she looks just sweet as a sugarplum. I'm sure you'll both do just fine." He gave me a wink and a smile.

I laughed lightly. "Thank you."

Just then, Carol came back out, wearing a yellow sundress and a matching hat, decorated with a yellow ribbon and golden flower. her hair was still wet, and still tied back in a bun. The rest of her clothes were stuffed into paper bags, which she carried on both arms. As we started through the doors, I took one of Carol's bags with one hand and waved the old man goodbye.

As he waved back and said "Come back and visit some time!" Only then I noticed that he was missing his left arm.

"Did you make a new friend?" Carol giggled at me.

I laughed. "Yeah, he's a veteran. He served with my dad, but retired after the battle against the Mouse King. That's when General Adian became Commander under my dad. Then my dad retired, and Aidan became General."

"And the other commanders?"

"Oh, they've been in their position for a long while. Commanders Packer and Manning are both older than General Aidan, I'm sure."

"Oh, wow. General Adian must be really good at his job."

"Yeah, he's a prodigy all right."

"What about Commander Woodlaine? General Aidan seems to be very close with them."

"Oh yeah," I adjusted my grip on Carol's bag. "They've known eachother since bootcamp, I think. So when Adian became General he promoted them to Commander when the other Commander retired."

"Do you think he would promote you to Commander?" Carol asked me.

I laughed at the very suggestion of it. "No, no. I haven't been in the workforce for nearly long enough to get promoted to anything yet."

"One day you will." Carol concluded.

"Maybe." I shrugged.

Eleven

It's Like Planning The Family Vacation

After I got back to base, Carol went to ask Fayola about her uniform. I got cleaned up and put my uniform on, then I found the rest of my team talking to each other outside of the meeting room.

"Ned! How did it go! Tell us everything!" Charles demanded.

"Where did you go?" Dante added.

"We went to a park. And yes, it went well." I answered.

"Do your pockets hurt?" Paris questioned.

"And why is your hair wet?" Charles continued.

With all of these incoming questions, I ignored Paris. "She pushed me into a lake," I laughed. "Is it too wet?"

"Too wet? Your hair is wet, Ned. Wet is wet." Charles sassed back at me.

"Whatever. It doesn't look bad, just don't let it drip onto your uniform or anything." Paris reassured me.

Fayola approached us and signed that she had just spoken to Carol, and that she enjoyed the date.

"That's great!" Dante said. "By the way, when is y'all's meeting?"

"It's in a few minutes, we should go ahead and go in though." I checked my watch. "On time is late and if you're late don't come." I quoted General Crixus-Wells.

"Yup." Paris stated, waving the team goodbye as she entered the door next to us.

I waved too as I followed her in. Turning around, I saw General Crixus-Wells, General Codagh, and Ravine in chairs at a long table. The Generals were on one side of the table next to each other, General Codagh closest to the head of the table. On the other side, across from General Crixus-Wells, was Ravine. Paris quickly took the seat next to Ravine on the side closest to the head of the table, and I sat next to General Crixus-Wells.

The tension boiled in the silent room between Ravine and I. The only noise was the ticking of a clock on the wall behind me. Ravine leaned forward carelessly, elbows resting on the table, hands folded together and supporting her chin. She had a grin as if she had a royal flush close to her chest. I sat upright, just like everyone else, thinking of something to say. Paris was the first to break the silence.

"Sir, do you know where General Aidan is?"

"No, I do not. I do know, however, that if he doesn't enter the room in the next thirty seconds, I'm snitching" General Crixus-Wells joked.

"To who?" Ravine inquired.

"Our King." General Codagh replied, arms crossed. She shot me a quick look, and it seemed that we were on the same wavelength.

Ravine leaned back and stretched her arm around Paris' chair. Paris froze, and just before Ravine could say anything smart, General Adian pushed through the door and sat at the head of the table. This apparently startled her, and she moved her arm to her lap.

General Aidan cleared his throat and slid four folders across the table to each of us.

"These are folders regarding information about the upcoming attack. Annotate it and I want it back by the end of the week." Aidan instructed.

Ravine lifted her head. "General, it's Thursday. How are we supposed to-"

"Ravine, if I wanted your opinion I would've asked." he shut her down. "But, you should be done first, since your folder has some restricted information. I want yours, Ravine, by end of day Friday."

Ravine huffed.

General Codagh spoke up. "Do you want ours on Saturday or Sunday?"

"If it isn't done Saturday I better have your folder at my door by the time I wake up Sunday." General Aidan answered. "Anyways, you two are here," he pointed at Paris and I. "because you're the only Cadets who've interacted with Ravine. When we eventually leave on ships, you three for sure will be on the same ship with me."

"How many people will be on each ship crew?" I asked.

Aidan patted his folder. "All in here." he turned to Generals Codagh and Crixus-Wells. "I asked you guys to be here because the King has asked that you two supervise training with the Christmas Spirit and Ravine. I don't have time today to go over the folder, so this meeting will be cut short. That's all I've got. Go to King Klaus with questions, not me."

Busily, we all stood up to leave, and as I started to trail behind everyone to leave after holding the door, General Aidan told me to stay.

"Yes sir?"

"I want to talk to you about your interview with Ravine."

"What do you mean, sir? I told you what she told me." *Shit.*

"B.S. I could see the whole thing Cadet. Give me the whole story." He crossed his arms- and even though we're similar in height he seemed to tower over me.

"Ravine gave me information as to why she chose to work with us, even though it doesn't have anything to do with what she wants to do. She just gave me her sob story, that's all." I just kept digging myself into a shithole.

"Don't lie to me, Nutcracker. She told you something else. I saw that you were pissed, and I wanna know why." Aidan pointed his finger at my chest.

With an almost annoyed breath, I spoke. "She told me about... a mistake she made. In the last ambush, she had a plan to help us win the war. She knew that we were drafting in able and willing veterans, so... so she made up some master plan to kill me and motivate my dad to lead us to victory. She bribed one of their troops to kill me and they killed the wrong Nutcracker." I sighed, feeling the weight lifted off my shoulders. I prayed Aidan wouldn't hate me forever because of this.

It was quiet for a moment. He was looking at the table for a minute or two before he said: "And that troop is the gargoyles you found surrounding him?"

"Yes sir."

"And they're dead?"

"Yes sir."

It was quiet for another minute, Aidan still staring at the table, I looked anywhere else.

"This isn't going to cause problems, is it?" He finally spoke again.

"What do you mean, Sir?"

"When we're on this boat, you aren't going to start anything with Ravine. Am I clear?"

"Yes sir."

He stood back upright. I couldn't tell if he was upset with the event or the outcome.

"Cadet Nutcracker?" General Aidan asked, looking me in the eye.

I prepared for the worst. "Yes Sir?"

"This isn't your fault."

That... wasn't what I expected him to say. "General I-"

"Nope. Not a word. None of this is your fault by any means. So don't overthink it and psych yourself out before this mission, because I know you, Nedrall."

"Y-yes Sir." I stuttered.

"You are dismissed." General Aidan backed up, and I left.

When I got back to my quarters, It was empty. Maybe Basil and Asam found something to do. I opened the file and began to look over it. There would be one or so teams on a ship. Generals and Commanders would disperse amongst them as they please. In this case, my team and I would be on the same ship as General Aidan and Commander Woodlaine. It seemed that Ravine and Carol would also be on our ship: The Royal Drosselmeyer. There was a map, with an updated route of travel once we reached the docks. It was pretty well hidden, and it led straight to the courtyard of the castle.

After a few hours of work and preparation passed, Charles confronted me with an offer. Paris had offered him first to go watch Carol and Ravine train, and he thought I'd like to go too. I agreed, and went with him.

"Did Ravine want to talk to you specifically just because she fought you when you were ten and lost?" Charles asked.

Here we go again. I knew better than to lie to Charles, too. "No. She said she felt guilty. Which she is."

"I knew it." Charles stopped walking and leaned against the wall. "What's up? What's she guilty of?"

"Am I that bad at keeping secrets?" I asked, rubbing the back of my head.

"Yes, Ned. You are. I thought you agreed you weren't gonna do this anymore?"

"Do what?"

"This! Keep secrets because you think nobody can or will help you! So you bottle all your fears and feelings up inside until you can blow up on the battlefield. It's what you do. Every time. Ned, It's okay to need help, alright? You don't have to do everything by yourself, you can't." Charles waved his hands around while he spoke.

"Is that really what I do?" I asked, dumbfounded.

"Yes, Ned! Now answer the damn question!" Charles demanded, loudly.

I was quiet for a moment. Charles and I had never argued over something serious before- ever. I didn't feel like I was keeping secrets from people because I didn't want their help. I just didn't want to burden them with my own issues. I didn't want to need help.

" ... She was supposed to kill me." I finally said.

Charles' face changed immediately. It went from annoyed and impatient to fear and regret. "I... She..."

"But her troop killed dad instead." I looked at Charles, tears welling in his eyes.

"Oh my God," Charles whispered, letting the tears flow from his eyes.

How my next words came out of my mouth was a mystery to me. But I just lost control of my mouth in the moment: "I wish they would've just killed me like they were supposed to-"

"Don't say that," Charles interrupted.

I continued. " Everyone would just be better off if I were dead. You, Aidan, Carol, the entire *country*." Before I knew it, tears streamed down my face, too.

"Stop it." Charles interrupted again.

"Aidan told me it couldn't have been my fault, but it really is, isn't it? All of this is my fault, all of it." I rambled on without thinking.

"Shut up!" Charles screamed. "Ned, listen to yourself! How could you have possibly known what Ravine's plan was? How could you have possibly known that? Do you think your father would let you stand here and cry as much as you have!? You are Nedrall *fucking* Nutcracker and you are one of the strongest, fastest, smartest, bravest soldiers in the whole damn workforce, and yet you think you're the scum of the Earth who doesn't deserve to be here. It's like you told Tyler! You worked damn hard to be here so you can't give up the chance you have, you understand!?"

I held my face in my hands and talked through them, muffledly. "You're right, I know. It's just- everything sucks lately and I feel like I have nothing to show for it."

"I know. But everything will get better. And you have Carol and Ravine to show for it. You got the Christmas Spirit on our side and because of you, we have a straightforward plan to win this war. You've gotta give yourself credit."

I peeked out from behind my fingers. "What would I do without you, Charles?" The tension dropped like a falling feather.

"I ask myself that every day. But actually promise me this time that you won't hide things anymore?"

"I promise."

For the first time in our lives, an uncomfortable silence hung over Charles and I as we walked to the arena. I heard the sounds of whips and explosions, followed by the faint sound of clapping. We entered, and from the bottom stand we could see General Codagh sparring with Ravine and General Crixus-Wells with Carol. To the other side, only a little higher in the stands, I saw Paris intently watching the spars. Well, one of them.

"I don't get how you and Paris scored so high in the love department." Charles nagged with a hint of jealousy. "I mean, I think I also deserve a magical prince in a green dress or iron armor."

Ignoring his envy, I questioned him. "Paris? What do you mean 'you and Paris'?" I knew Ravine was into Paris, but Paris hadn't talked that much about Ravine, had she?

"You seriously haven't noticed, Ned? Paris has kept her eye on Ravine ever since she got here. Why else do you think Paris-scared-of-everything-Fabron asked General Crixus to work with Ravine, of all people?"

"She asked?" Apparently I was more out of the loop than I thought. When we got up to the stands, I finally connected the dots. "You weren't nervous putting the clips on Ravine because you were scared, you were nervous because you think she's cute!" I poked fun at her.

"What are you talking about? Charles, you snitch!" She kicked her feet out at him, but they didn't extend very far.

"You would look like a little kid standing next to Ravine." I joked.

"So? At least Ravine hasn't accidentally tried to drown me."

Charles failed to hide his snicker.

"Carol didn't drown me, she got water in my ear. What did she tell you?" I corrected. "And the only reason that happened was because I actually went on a date with her."

"Does this mean we need to set up Paris and Ravine?" Charles smirked at Paris and I.

"Maybe." I shrugged.

"NO!" Paris brought her hands up to her face, which was turning red.

Laughing at Paris, I turned to watch the two in combat. Carol was clearly giving General Crixus-Wells a run for his money. Ravine and Codagh, not so much. It would help Ravine if she knew how to land on her feet. It seemed her fighting hadn't changed a bit since I'd last seen her. On the other hand, Carol probably had experience defending herself.

Out of nowhere, we heard General Codagh yell "Heads up!"

Hardly a moment later the three of us dove from a stray ornament-grenade that Ravine had misfired. No one was injured, Ravine seemed to be using smaller, less serious explosives for training combat.

There were multiple small groups scattered across the stands, who all wanted to watch the two of them train; I thought they would be looking at the explosion, but it happened that Ravine was flying towards us, so she caught their attention instead. Ravine landed on the stands not-so-gracefully, which made me remember how she landed in the forest all those years ago. She still couldn't land on her feet. Not surprisingly, her attention went first to Paris.

"Are you hurt?" Ravine asked her.

"We're good, thanks." I responded, dusting the ash from the explosion off my sleeve. Charles looked at me from behind Ravine but didn't say anything.

"I'm okay, but y'know, if you aim your grenades at where you think her sword will go, then when she moves it, it will reflect off the sword and explode right there. Instead of throwing them at her, where she can dodge." Paris advised.

"Thanks, I'll try it." Ravine flew off, again landing messily on the arena floor.

"No yeah," Charles started, quickly erasing the tension. "Ravine definitely has a thing for you, Paris."

"You think so?" Paris asked.

"Yeah, but I think she's scared of General Aidan." I added.

"I noticed that too." Paris stood up. "At the meeting, she put her arm on my chair but took it back when Adian walked in the room. She's usually more confident than that- more carefree."

I bit my lip, wanting to snicker at the use of the word confident, but I didn't.

"She did that? Ooh, we've got to set you up!" Charles exclaimed, stomping his feet on the stands.

"Where is Fayola and Dante?" I wanted to steer as far away from this conversation as possible. Anything and everything about Ravine irked me in the wrong direction.

"They're training somewhere else," Charles answered.

"We should go get them. General Aidan is going to go over a plan with our group." I stated.

"When did he say that?" Paris turned around and asked me.

"After you all left the meeting." I answered, and stood up from the bleachers.

Paris led the way back to the main building of base, and by led the way I mean she ran and we sprinted to keep up. We would've told her to slow down, but we were too out of breath to say anything, much less actually breathe.

As we approached base and finally slowed down, Charles caught his breath before I did, so he could tell Paris how much of a speed-demon she is. It was only after Paris responded with an embarrassed giggle that I caught my breath. I regained my posture, somehow forgetting how much taller I am than Paris and Charles. It seemed that if there were to be a crowd I'd be the one looking over heads- which wasn't a difficult task in hindsight, since Fayola might be the tallest person in the kingdom aside from King Klaus.

We split up, Paris went searching for Dante and Charles and I went looking for Fayola. We walked through the many halls of the maze that our king calls "Capitol Base". After we turned many corners, we finally found Fayola ducking under a doorway to leave her room.

As soon as she waved at us, we heard light footsteps tapping quickly down the halls, and heavier ones going slower. By the time we could turn around to see what the commotion was, Paris was running down the hall toward us. Dante was following far behind her.

"Paris you take every moment you can to let us know you're fast, huh?" Charles told her.

"Hey, he wanted to race me." Paris turned to Dante as he finally caught up.

"What the hell, man? How is it even possible to go that fast when you're so small?" Dante caught his breath.

After the laughter died down, we all went back to the meeting room I left almost an hour ago. Fayola opened the door to find General Aidan sitting at the head of the table, looking through the folder he gave us a while ago, with three others sitting at his side. We sat down at the table.

"Alright," he started. "Your guys' team as well as Tyler's team- or what's left of it- has a slightly different route of action, so I'm gonna talk with you guys first because you're least likely to give me a headache."

Dante looked confused. "Sir, with all due respect, why us?"

General Aidan closed his folder and looked at us. "Look at yourselves. You guys have the most raw talent of any of the teams we have. You're fast, smart, strong, skilled, and, again, least likely to give me a headache."

Charles spoke up. "So why is Tyler's team doing this?"

Aidan sighed. "Jackasses as they are, that team also has some strong soldiers,"

Fayola looked worried- unsure of herself. To General Aidan, she signed, 'But Sir, the last time we were out on a battlefield, I was taken by a gargoyle almost as soon as they attacked us.'

Aidan interrupted her: "No, no," his hands waved across the table as if swiping Fay's thoughts from the air. "This is your problem. All of you. You don't trust yourselves. That's what'll kill you. Your teammates trust you, I'm trusting you, hell- even the king trusts you all with this task."

Aidan leaned over the table and looked at each of us.

"You are not here because I am asking you to take on this task. You are here because you *will* take on this task. You all are ready. If you weren't, I wouldn't be wasting my breath right now."

Fayola sat up straight, like a tower. She nodded, and a "Yes Sir," came from the rest of us.

General Aidan backed off of the table, and the tension lifted. I looked at Charles, his face looked like stone, staring at the table. I watched Paris' chest rise with a breath but stayed puffed when she exhaled. Dante kept his fists on the table silently.

General Aidan laid a map of the gargoyle's kingdom out on the table in front of all of us. Displayed on the field in front of the port we'd be entering through was a mass of dots.

"Those dots are teams of other soldiers," He put down a black and a white knight chess piece in front of the dots, as if they were leading them. "The black piece is Commander Woodlaine, and the White piece is myself."

He put a black knight on the right side of the map in the front of the attack. "Commander Packer," He put another one on the mirrored side of Packer. "And Commander Manning."

"Where will we be, Sir?" Dante asked.

He placed two white pawn pieces next to Commander Packing and Commander Manning. "Right here. You guys will be with Commander Packer."

"Why aren't we with you pushing through the middle? Isn't that the fastest way to the castle?" I asked, analyzing the pieces.

"Your team specifically will go the long way around into the front courtyard of the castle from the side. Through the middle is fastest, but I sit on that white horse in the front. That paints a bright target and draws their attention."

Charles rubbed his chin with understanding. "So while you, Commander Woodlaine, and the rest of the teams fight in this field, we're gonna go around the side into the courtyard?"

"Yes," General Aidan answered.

Fayola asked if Tyler's team would meet us in the courtyard.

"No, not exactly." He changed the pieces to show where we would be. He moved our pawn piece into the courtyard, and left Commander Packer just outside the wall. On the opposite side of the courtyard, Commander Manning was on the outside of that wall and Tyler's pawn piece sat on the bridge that connected the first wall and the front wall to the courtyard.

"They'll be just outside the walls," He explained. "To keep any gargoyles out, innocent or otherwise."

There was one piece that didn't fit though. And as if she'd stolen the thought from my brain, Paris asked where Ravine would be in all of this.

"General Codagh's got dibs on Ravine for the duration of the battle, so you'll need to ask her. She will be on the ship with us though," Aidan sighed. "So that Codagh doesn't kill Ravine on the way there. General Crixus-Wells may know what she'll do on the field, but I generally don't care. I trust General Crixus-Wells to keep her in line."

Once again, Aidan backed off of the table. "Anything else you guys need to know?"

We all looked at each other, all were satisfied.

"No, we're ready," I answered.

"I know." Aidan said.

Twelve

Hello, Sailor

Half an hour until we left the dock. I was searching for Carol. All I could see for the past half hour were helmets, bustling back and forth. It was very early, but the team had already met up, and Paris told me Carol was looking for me, too. Everyone was hustling to their ships, but I had to find her. Pushing through the crowds, I managed to open a door. I got outside where it was slightly calmer. Through a window, across the yard I could see her strapping armor to herself. She saw me approaching and opened the door before I could knock.

"Wow, it's busy out there, huh?" Carol sighed, tightening a buckle across her waist.

"Yeah, you wouldn't believe how long it took for me just to get through the hall," I laughed.

"You don't look very ready to me, sir," She did not sympathize with me.

"I'm not, I had to see you first." I rubbed the back of my head and the room.

She smiled. "That's very sweet of you, but I'm coming with you, Ned."

"You are? Oh! Right! You are."

"Yes, silly. Why do you think I'm putting all this on? For show?"

"Right, shoot, then I gotta go get ready," I started back for the door in a hurry but before I could grab the handle, Carol caught my hand.

She pulled me in, and kissed me on the cheek. "Go get 'em, Sailor."

All I could do was smile to myself as I left. I hurried to my quarters to pull my things from the closet. Luckily, I had packed them all up after the meeting the previous night and all I had to do was put on my armor- which didn't take very long. Everyone I was roomed with had most likely already gotten to their ships. Zooming out of my room, there were less people than before. I jogged more than walked through the halls, and eventually made it outside. There, I ran to the docks. Metal clunked with every step. I got out of breath fast, carrying so much armor and luggage.

Finally, I broke the treeline and found the beach. I was faced with the surprisingly simple task of finding my ship out of hundreds- all I had to do was find the ship with the white horse.

General Aidan went just about anywhere he could with his horse on base, meaning he would probably wait until the very last minute before he took his horse to the livestock carrier. I walked down the beach to find it, because there was no way in hell I was running down the beach with this much weight on. Was I trained for this in boot camp? Sure. Did that mean I had to do it right now? No. Eventually I found it: The Royal Drosselmeyer. I boarded it, and quickly found everyone in the crew: Commander Packer, General Adian, Ravine, my team, and Carol. Going down into the cabin I found my cot behind a curtain and set my luggage, helmet, and armored boot covers under it then ran back up to the deck to greet everyone.

"Look who showed up!" Dante welcomed me with a hug. He looked more intimidating in his armor, and it threw me for a loop.

Approaching from behind was equally as intimidating Fayola. Them standing next to each other was nostalgic of when we first met. The memory shot up through me and all I could do was smile. The moment was broken when Charles jumped on me from behind.

"Charles-!" I tried to keep myself from falling, because I knew he would crash down with me.

He let go of me and started laughing- so did Dante.

"Charles, you're gonna have to start being more careful where you jump once we get to open water." I glared at him.

"Why?' Dante asked, curious but still laughing at me. "Ropes hang off the ship for a reason and we won't hit any storms anyways!"

"The ocean could be as still as a pool and Charles would still drown!" I shot Charles another look.

Charles crossed his arms. "Just because I can't swim doesn't mean I'll die on a boat. I won't have to swim if I stay on the boat."

"Keep talking, I'll put floaties on you." I cut back.

"Wait, Charles, You don't know how to swim?" Dante asked. Fayola looked just as stunned.

"No, but it's no big deal. I can learn anytime." He replied, putting his hand on his hip.

"You've been saying that since we were ten." I added.

"Whatever"

Fayola signed: 'I am willing to retrieve him if he falls.' with her soft, small smile.

Charles laughed a little. "Thanks, Fay. But I'll be fine." He said, looking at me like I'm worrying too much.

I sighed, then realized we're missing a team member. "Where's Paris?"

"In the Cabin, probably flirting with Ravine." Charles remarked.

"And Carol?"

"She's not here yet," Dante cocked his head. "You takin' roll call or something?"

"Just curious, I guess."

Then, General Aidan and Commander Woodlaine boarded the ship. They were one hundred times scarier fully armored than in full uniform. They didn't even look at us as they set up the ship, preparing it to set sail.

The only acknowledgement we received was "Five minutes 'till we're out," from Commander Woodlaine.

We dispersed, all doing something to prep the ship. Once everything was in order and there was fuel in the engine, we were set off into the unknown.

Only after everything was done did Ravine come up to say hi. She strutted in her new armor as if she was on a cruise ship. Remembering what Aidan had warned me about and me simply not caring enough to give her attention, I walked right past her down into the body of the ship. I figured I might look for Carol, someone I would have much rather come up to deck.

At that moment it hit me that I hadn't seen her on the deck at all since I left her at base. I knew she'd probably gotten to the ship before me but it didn't feel right that she didn't come up to help or even say hi.

After searching for a while, I finally found her in her 'room' if you can even call it that. She had taken most of her armor off and was wearing the red uniform that had been given to her, it looked just like the rest of ours. Hair was tied back messily and she looked pale, especially for someone that literally glowed all the time.

"Hey, are you hiding from the rest of us for something?" I joked, but I could tell something was off.

"Just a bit seasick is all. And don't think that I don't know that you came down here to get away from Ravine."

"Didn't know spirits could get seasick." I laughed.

"Am I right though? Did you?"

"Yeah.. but mostly to find you." I sat on the floor next to her cot.

"You can't avoid her forever, Ned. Especially not here."

"I know," I groaned.

"I know you hate her, but you have to work with her. everything depends on it."

"Right, almost forgot."

"Sorry."

I stopped for a moment. I liked how the silence felt comfortable. Like the quietness wasn't heavy, it was just us there. I imagined what it would have been like if dad would have been able to meet Carol. They are both so gentle and warm-hearted.

"He would've really liked you, y'know?"

"You think so?" She rolled over to face me. A little color had come back to her face.

"You both are kind-of exactly the same. Kind-hearted and peaceful, but strong."

"You always get a certain look on your face when you talk about him. Your jaw clenches more and you narrow your eyes like you're squinting"

"I think I'm just squinting because you're bright." I joked, and she laughed like she'd never heard a joke before. "We should go back up, if you feel better."

"Let's get Paris, too." She sat up. "I think she fell asleep after how little sleep she got last night and all the running around she did this morning."

"Sounds par for the course."

"We'll meet you up there."

Carol left to find Paris, and when I got back up to deck, General Aidan and Commander Packer weren't present- most likely steering the ship in the control room. The rest of the team were having a good time, watching Ravine to party tricks in the sky. I took a deep breath, allowing the fact that I was going to have to be the bigger person resonate within me.

"Ned!" Charles waved. "Where've ya been?"

"Went to find Carol and Paris. They're on their way up now."

Ravine landed on the taffrail of the ship, swaying it noticeably but not too much that we could fall. "Glad you could join us," She lifted her head up to me and smiled.

"Glad to be here," I responded with a sigh.

"Ravine, you're so lucky you get the whole open sky to yourself out here, while we're stuck on this boat. Man, if I could fly you'd never see me again," Dante laughed.

"What-ever." Charles split the word in half, for emphasis. "Solid ground is just where I like it." Charles tapped his foot on the deck of the ship. "No risk of falling to my impending doom down here."

"You're not on solid ground," Ravine stated.

"Exactly, what if you fall off the boat?" I egged him on.

"Oh shove it, Ned," Charles said, ironically shoving me in response. He rolled his eyes.

"Y'know, Dante, I can lift you up and you'd get to see everything I get to see." Ravine relaxed her wings at her side.

Before Dante replied, we heard the screech of the cabin door swinging open behind us. Paris and Carol stepped through.

"Hi!" Paris waved, adding many i's to the end of her greeting.

"Hello!" Carol followed.

"Hey," I turned to them. "Dante was just about to get a lift from Ravine."

"Really?" asked Paris.

Dante's cheeks turned a shade of red. "Do you think you could lift me though? I mean, I'm a pretty big guy."

"Tch-," Ravine shrugged, promptly flying at him and grabbing him around his biceps with her talons. A noise of surprise left his mouth but not one of fear. Looking up at him, I could almost feel again the feeling of being torn from the ground by a gargoyle. Reaching any limb I could towards the ground, hoping anything or anyone would pull me back down. But here I was, watching Dante have the time of his life being flung around like a ragdoll by a gargoyle. Instinctively, my hands wrapped around my opposite arm's bicep as if I were protecting myself from nothing.

When he landed- or more accurately fell- onto the boat, Ravine perched onto the taffrail of the boat swaying it again ever so slightly. Only then did I notice Carol at my side, closer than people normally stand next to others. She was also looking at Dante, and didn't notice me seeing her.

Again, there was the screech of the door to the lower deck. Out of it came Commander Woodlaine.

"Why on God's green earth is Ravine flying Dante around?"

All of us looked at eachother, wondering the same thing: how did they see that?

"We can't do that, sir?" Dante asked, looking like he'd seen a ghost.

"*No*, Cadet Garcia. You may *not* fly above deck under *any* circumstances," They declared. Their glare shifted to Ravine. "That goes for you too." The door screeched shut again. Ravine's expression changed from lightheartedness to resentment in a snap. We all gave a "Yes sir,"

It was quiet for a moment or two, we all just looked around at each other with faces that read 'So what now?'

"Well," Charles broke the silence. "I'm gonna check out the lower deck, if you guys wanna join me." As he left, the only people that didn't follow were Carol, Ravine, Paris, and myself.

"Well, then," Ravine turned away from the door back to the group.

"I wonder why they're so strict about that," Paris crossed her arms.

"Yeah," Carol started, " I'm glad I didn't fly before they said something."

All eyes turned to Carol. "You can fly?" I asked

"Well, yes, but I prefer the ground. It's very tiring to be in the air."

"That's true," Ravine confirmed. "I guess I've just done it so much my muscles have gotten used to it.

"The muscles in your wings," Paris said, waiting for Ravine to verify her response.

"Right,"

"Then how does Carol fly?" Paris implored, gesturing to Carol.

"I... I don't know," Carol tilted her head and examined her arms in front of her, as if she would find the answer written on her. "I just do it, I never learned how. It's as second nature to me as walking is."

"Huh," Paris looked dumbfounded. I didn't think she'd wrapped her head around magic yet.

"If your people could use magic the war would probably be over, assuming there was ever a chance of it starting." Ravine stated.

Paris looked up at her with a curiosity different from how she normally looks.

"What made you come here?" Paris questioned, very matter-of-fact.

I tried my best not to look like I already knew, but the fact that my focus constantly switched from Ravine to Paris and back to Ravine didn't help much.

Ravine looked at her, like Paris' newfound confidence didn't surprise or bother her. She rolled her shoulders back with a smirk.

"Same as you all," Ravine said smoothly. "I want you to win."

"But why?" Paris edged on. "I mean, everyone's a bit curious."

I continued to watch uncomfortably. Carol looked like she was holding a bubble in her mouth, eyes pointed anywhere but Paris and Ravine.

"I had a different plan before," Ravine's eyes moved to me for a split second. "But I messed it up, bad. And now I'm here trying to fix it."

fix it? Did she just say fix it?

That phrase infuriated me. Fix what? A death? A lack thereof? She said it as if it was just a favor to make up. As if she could just make it up to me for being the reason my dad died in my arms. And just when I thought she wasn't going to be such a hassle.

Paris looked at me, then back at Ravine, as if she understood now that I had something to do with that reason, but not that it wasn't any of her business.

"So what's going on?" Paris continued to interrogate with her chin held high. She really didn't know when to stop, did she?

Ravine finally bit her tongue. I balled my hand into a fist, not violently, but I was angry. Carol countered it by taking hold of my hand.

"Listen, Paris," I tried to figure out how to say this calmly, knowing Paris was sensitive. "It's not something I want you in the middle of. It's just a lot of crap, I didn't even want Charles in it."

Paris finally listened, I think.

"Okay," She said. "I know I'm bad about butting in, I'm sorry."

General Aidan saved me from having to say something in response. The familiar squeal of the door sent a flood of relief over me.

"Cadet Nutcracker, come with me." He stated, not waiting for my response as he turned back around and went down the stairs. Without a word, I followed him. I couldn't see the reaction of anyone behind me, but I could assume.

General Aidan walked very fast and with purpose. We didn't share any words as he led me into a room. I minded my head as I made my way under the doorframe and he shut the door behind me. I turned around to face him and he looked uncomfortable. Like he didn't even want to be there talking to me.

"Yes sir?" Was the only thing I could think to say.

"I just got done talking with Commander Woodlaine," He started. "And we both agreed that this is something you'll want to hear."

"Yes?" I braced myself.

"I know that you probably felt.. or still feel.. like you should have been the one to die instead of your father." He finally said.

The words crashed into me like a truck. I swallowed back the shock and let him continue.

"I need you to know that's not true." He seemed more comfortable and genuine now. He was right, but what's true or not didn't change how I felt. "I need you to know that because I have felt that way before. You cannot let those feelings take over your mind, especially not now."

"What?" I was so confused. In all my life of watching Aidan by my father's side and in his leadership, I'd never hear him reveal himself like this. "What do you mean?"

"When I was around your age, I made this same trip we're making now. I went on a ship with your father, my team, and a few other teams for an attack on the border. When we got there, my team and I got ambushed. I was the only survivor."

I stood there, frozen. I didn't know what to say or what this story was leading up to, but honestly I was too shook up from it to respond.

"After it happened, I thought I should've died with them. But your father told me something that day and I believe it is the sole reason I have the role I have today."

"What did he say?" I longed for any word of advice I could get from my dad. It was ironic how his constant training and advice annoyed me when I was younger, but I would do it all over again now.

"He told me that I was the last piece of them left alive. He told me to live in their memory: to be a walking monument to their names."

Again, I was left speechless, unable to think of a response that could match the sincerity of what he'd just told me.

"I can't stand in the place your father held, I know that, and I debated myself a lot on whether or not I should even say anything, but I ended up deciding you should know," He stood up straight, and looked me in the eye. He put his hand on my shoulder, like my dad used to do to him and I so often. "Nedrall, live as a walking, breathing monument to your father. And I'll try to do the same."

His voice shook at the end. I knew my father meant a lot to him as well, but I never knew just how much. "I will, Sir. Thank you."

He started to leave, assumingly with nothing left to say.

"For what it's worth," I started. He turned and waited for me to finish. "I think you're doing a really good job."

Thirteen

So Nobody Was Gonna Tell Me?

The next morning, the air felt different. Everyone seemed unaware of the fact that we're going to war. Everything was light and cheerful, like we were on a family cruise vacation. I think some more sleep did everyone a lot of good. Yesterday's events still hung over me like mistletoe, if mistletoe was poison ivy.

The rations we brought could hardly be called food. It was the most flavorless, dry, revolting breakfast I'd ever eaten. I suppose I'd grown up with grand dining my whole life. General Aidan, Commander Packer, and Ravine seemed less bothered than the rest of us.

But Charles hated it most of all: he'd barely even picked up his spoon.

It was just Charles and I eating together. I didn't want to eat whatever this was, but I knew I had to. Charles, however, was more stubborn.

"Well, you have to eat something," I tried to persuade him.

"I'd rather jump off the boat and eat whatever fish I find," Charles has a seafood allergy and can't swim.

I laughed. He'd always been this picky when it came to food. "Well what did you expect we'd eat, huh?"

"Not mush," He said, lifting some of it with his spoon and proceeded to watch it fall off of his spoon with a gross look.

I'd finally choked down the last bit of my food. It was a horrible experience, but at least it was over, until the next meal.

"Just hold your nose and choke it down, you won't taste it," I explained.

"Ugh, fine," Charles pinched his nose and shut his eyes tight. Hastily, he shoveled the food into his mouth.

I stood up, getting bored of watching Charles eat. "I'm gonna go find the others,"

"Okay, I'm just gonna be here recovering," He responded, as if he'd already gotten food poisoning. He definitely didn't.

As I shut the door behind me, I made my way up to the deck. The sun was just now rising. I assumed the others were up, just haven't woken up enough yet to socialize. Except for General Aidan and Commander Woodlaine, of course. I leaned over the rail, looking into the sunrise that reflected off the water. This was the first time I'd been alone in months. I looked around, and there was nothing but open water for miles. I wondered if things would get more dangerous as we got closer to enemy territory. Probably, but hey, that's why we were there, right?

Just one more day on this boat. One more day, one more night, and then we're there. I looked out ahead of the ship, squinting at the sun's orange radiation on the horizon.

"That's where the end is." I thought. *"Somewhere over that way, there are thousands of people who want me dead."*

The screech of the cabin door halted my thoughts. I turned around, and even if I hadn't, the scrapes of Ravine's wings against the doorframe would have given her away.

"What are you doing up here?" She asked.

"Not watching Charles choke down those God-awful rations, that's what," I joked.

"I was actually looking for you," She stepped next to me and looked quietly out into the water.

"Why?" I looked at her but her stare didn't waver.

"Before we get too close to Gargoyle lines, I need to warn you," She straightened her posture. "King Khelbent wants you dead, specifically. And without your father, you're just as vulnerable as Carol now."

"Everyone's vulnerable right now," I replied. I didn't exactly know what she meant by that.

She looked at me, almost confused. "Yes, but you and Carol most of all. With your powers combined, he plans to enslave the world,"

"What?" I knew my family name was infamous, but to go as far as saying we had some kind of power seemed a bit much.

Her look of confusion turned to some kind of fear. "What?" she asked back.

"I don't have any power, I'm nothing special just because of my dad, Ravine. I'm just like anyone else,"

She just stared at me, biting her nails... claws? Nails. As I noticed her posture becoming more uncomfortable, I saw her sharp nails and teeth. I'd almost forgotten for a second that I didn't trust Ravine.

"Nedrall," Ravine started. "General Aidan didn't tell you? He told me, so I assumed you knew too."

"General Aidan? What? Ravine, I think I'd know if I had any magic," I asserted. At this point, I was trying to make sense of this confusion. Then, out of the back of my mind, came a memory.

"You're more like that girl than you know, you'll figure it out."

Is this what that meant? If Aidan knew, why wouldn't he tell me? Something wasn't adding up, and I needed to figure it out.

"What is it?" Ravine could tell I knew something.

"Don't say anything about this conversation to General Aidan," I ordered.

"Uhm, okay?" She looked at the door, then back at me. "Did you really not know?"

"Not really," I started. Immediately, I felt a load of guilt and disappointment drop over me. Not only should I have known to figure this out, but Aidan should have told me. "I should have been able to figure this out a long time ago, though,"

I left Ravine on the deck. Pacing through the tight halls of the lower deck, my mind raced ten times faster. It's always something new, there's always some new shit going on. I marched up to the captain's cabin door, I raised my fist up-

and I put it back down. I realized I should think things through before I go arguing with General Aidan. Apparently the universe thought not, because just then I heard footsteps approaching from my right.

"Cadet Nutcracker, is there a reason you're standing there staring at the door?" It was General Adian.

"No Sir!" I saved, unsmoothly. I walked briskly away. Oh God. Oh no oh no oh no, don't do this right now. Aidan's words stopped me in my tracks.

"Cadet, what do you want?" he demanded more than asked.

"Nothing, sir, I zoned out is all," I lied.

"No you didn't."

"No, I didn't," Shit. I guess this is happening now.

"So, what do you want?" His eyes were focused on me, like black holes ready to swallow me whole. He stood as still as a statue in his uniform. To this day, he was the most intimidating man I'd ever met.

"Do I have magic? I'm sure I don't, but-"

"Why? Where did you hear that?" His posture didn't change but his eyes grew interrogative.

I swallowed back my fear. "Ravine told me, Sir." I stated, still on the presumption that she was right. She could've been messing with me, for some reason. But what would be her reason? Was trying to get into my head to betray us? To try to get me to turn on Aidan? If she was really right, then how did I not know? How did so many people other than myself know I had magic and never bothered to tell *me*?

Aidan inhaled, much like a parent does when their child does something wrong and messes everything up. "Come inside, Cadet." He opened the door I'd just been staring at and gestured me to go inside. He followed me in and shut the door behind us.

"Before you say anything," Aidan started, "I didn't tell you because your father told me not to."

"What?" So, it was true, I had some form of magic. It must suck, since it hasn't been obvious that I have it. Why would my dad hide it from me? Why the hell did Ravine know?

"I know you have a lot of questions, but just listen to me first. Your dad wanted you to find out for yourself but that hasn't happened yet. Honestly, I'm surprised it didn't happen when he-" He stopped.

"When he died?" I finished for him. That's why he said I was like Carol. He must've thought that when he was dying. *Why isn't it happening yet?*. Immediately, I couldn't help but feel like a failure. My father died hoping I'd gain some wild power and I didn't. He expected me to become something I needed to be to save him, and I didn't. I can't help that I didn't, but that doesn't change the fact that he died because of me not doing something. All this time I thought it was just Ravine's fault but I was just as guilty as her now.

"I know it's a lot to take in, especially right now, but I know it will happen," Aidan broke my train of thought.

"How could you know that?"

"Because it happened to your father, too."

"What?" Too many things were happening. Too much all at once.

"It was the day he killed the Mouse King. He said he saw a spirit charged with power and he didn't know what it was, but it gave him a strength greater than anything else alive. He said he felt like he could topple over kingdoms and overthrow the greatest of tyrants. But, out of that magic, came you. No one knows how, but when it was all said and done, Navid left the battlefield with you in his arms. That's why he retired early, and that's why he couldn't use his god-like strength anymore."

"Because it's in me now," I looked down at my hands, then back up at Adian.

"You know, that's why he always expected so much of you, when you were little," He crossed his arms in a relaxed position. "He knew what you were capable of."

"Yeah, and I wasn't capable of shit when I could have saved him. None of us would be standing here right now if Ravine or I could just do what we were supposed to do the first fucking time." I looked down at the floor and held my breath, as if I was holding all my guilt inside of me.

Aidan grinned and laughed quietly. "Cadet, if everyone did what they were supposed to all the time, we wouldn't really be living, we'd just be following orders,"

"Says the General," I grinned back. I remembered the day I first met Aidan. I couldn't remember how old I was, but I remembered seeing an anxious, awkward twenty-something year old with too much talent for his own good. Looking up, I realized he was just the same family friend he was before.

"Well, you still have to follow my orders," he said on his way out.

Before he left, I had one last question. "General Adian, do you know who gave my dad his powers?"

"No, but I can assure you it was something much more powerful than Carol, if that's what you were wondering,"

"Right," I knew that. When I met Carol when I was a kid, she was a kid too. There was no way she gave my dad magic and made me. Did that mean there was another spirit more powerful than Carol? I remembered my dad telling me stories about it, but I couldn't remember them, they were so long ago.

General Aidan and I dispersed from the captain's room, and I headed straight to Carol. I was tired of surprises, and I was basically expecting them at this point. I just wanted to clear the air as soon as possible so I wouldn't go and screw up the whole plan and cost another life. I couldn't go through that again.

Her curtain was pulled slightly back, so I let myself in. She was sitting on her cot, fiddling with a potted plant. Upon closer inspection, I saw that she was using magic to make it dance.

"Hello Ned," She greeted warmly.

"Hi Carol," I closed the door behind me and sat on the end of the bed, rather awkwardly.

"Is there something you need?" She stopped playing with the plant and looked over at me. Her expression always seemed so gentle, she always looked like she was listening carefully.

Her chlorokinesis distracted me. "You can do things with plants?"

"Oh, yeah." Carol put down the plant. "I can use magic with most elements."

"Is that how you can create trees?"

"Well, it's more like turning another living thing into a tree. Usually a plant- like a blade of grass- but I've also had to use it in self-defense before."

"Against gargoyles?"

"Yeah. I feel horrible when I do it, but it's the only thing I can do to stop them that isn't painful."

"They're only puppets, not real people. You're good at this magic thing, huh?"

"I guess you could say that."

"That's actually kind-of what I wanted to talk to you about." I rubbed the back of my head.

"What do you mean?" Carol looked up at me from her cot.

"So... I just learned something... new," I started. "Apparently, I can use magic? Or I am magic? I don't know how any of this works, but I know I was made from magic. So-" I began to trail off in confusion.

"So you came to me for help?" Carol finished my sentence.

"Yeah. I don't even know what I'm supposed to be able to do, much less how to do it,"

"You'll be able to do it when you need to. That's how it always goes. you won't be able to force your magic to happen the first time, it will come to you."

"How convenient."

Normally, I'd be excited to learn that I could control magic. But this whole situation just annoyed me. There always had to be something special about me, something different. Since the day I was born- or I guess created- I'd been told I was special and destined for great things. I didn't want to be special, I just wanted to be. I'd never gotten to just exist peacefully, no, I'd be the cause of my father's death, I'd learn a secret kept from me for years, I'd become magic.

I supposed that's why King Khelbent wanted Carol and I so bad.

Hell, Carol's magic alone would be enough to bring us down, much less whatever I could do as well.

"Hey, don't think about it too much. I know It's a lot, especially growing up without it, but I know you'll do great." Carol rested her hand on mine.

"Thanks, I guess I'm just tired of things changing." I admitted. "I'm tired of being the one who's supposed to fix things or be special."

"Take it from me," She moved a little closer to me. "Being magic isn't so bad. And, once this is all over, you never have to fight or use magic again."

That's what happened to dad. That's how he got his fame, and he lived the rest of his life in luxury. His kid, supposedly destined to be just as strong and powerful and magical, would give a life under pressure to be the best. A child destined to be born from magic and destined to die in it, probably.

"I'll make sure of that," I promised. To myself, sure, but also to my future children. They wouldn't be destined for glory, they'd be kids. They'd be my kids, and if everything goes well, they'll probably be spoiled to all hell, but they'll get to be themselves.

Carol leaned into me. I guess she took the silence of my thoughts as some kind of snuggle-sign. I didn't stop her; I was always having some existential crisis to think about anyways.

That opened the way to the next thought that invaded my head: would I even have kids? Would I live past this week to have them? Would Carol live past this week to have them? If both of us lived, would my kid be made from magic too? Would I have a say in the matter? There were so many questions I had, all of them dad could answer.

Carol must've been able to tell that I was getting worked up, because she smacked my leg with the back of her hand and said, "I told you not to worry. Seriously, you're going to be okay. Whatever happens, you'll always have me, your team, and the rest of us. We're here for you, Ned."

"You guys have been the only consistent, normal thing about any of this. I don't want that to change."

"It won't."

Fourteen

Think Battleships, But
Less Fun

It was the next morning when I met Ravine on the deck again.

"Sorry about yesterday, I didn't mean to mess anything up, really. I thought you knew. Believe me, Aidan raised some hell to me about it." She apologized.

"I needed to figure it out at some point in time anyways," Something about Ravine still infuriated me. She was always behind whatever surprises screwed up my life. Not being an asshole to her was better for everyone at this point, though.

I'd told Charles already what I'd found out- I told him after I talked to Carol. He was far more excited about it than I was. We both agreed that I needed to tell the team, which was something I still hadn't done.

As if my thought willed it into existence, Dante, Fayola, Paris, and Charles stepped onto deck. The group was being awkwardly rushed up the stairs by Charles, who was looking at me like how my dad would when he wanted me to apologize to someone- usually for something irrelevant, mind you.

"Go on, Ned. You said you'd tell them today." Charles put his hands on his hips in a very hurry-it-up manner. Everyone, including Ravine, looked confused and here I was, looking like I was holding a secret from them.

"Uh, yeah," I started. Everyone was looking at me and I couldn't help but start to fiddle with my own hands. "Supposedly- it hasn't happened yet- but supposedly I have magic. I don't know what specifically I can do or how to use it, but Carol said it just happens at some opportune time. After that happens, well, I don't know what happens after that."

"Oh," Paris laughed with relief. "I thought you were gonna say something bad. Like that you were sick or injured or something wo-."

"Magic?! You can use magic?!" Dante interrupted. He made fists with his hands to try and contain his excitement.

"Not yet, I don't know when I can actually use it." I corrected, looking down at my hands. I was still fiddling with them.

Fayola signed to me, 'I'm sure you'll do great.' with a smile. She never has much to add to conversations, but she always manages to say something kind.

That was when I noticed it: Paris, Ravine, and Fayola all had matching twin braids. Paris' hair had grown out a bit since I'd met her- it used to be just at her shoulders and now she can tie it back into a ponytail. It was braided back on her scalp into the ponytail she was wearing. Fayola and Ravine had almost identical braids, probably since their hair was equally as long.

"When did this happen?" I asked, rotating to point at each of them. I was always good at changing the subject from me. It's an art you learn when everyone knows who you are but doesn't know anything about you.

"Fayola's really good at doing hair. We kinda had a girls' night after I gave you an existential crisis." Ravine joked.

"Charles tried to get in, but we wouldn't let him." Paris added, her eyes looked cuttingly at Charles.

"You guys just can't handle my hair," Charles snarked.

"You're not a girl!" replied Paris, equally as snarky.

"He decided to hang out with me afterwards," Dante added. "He couldn't find Ned anywhere." He gave me a suggestive look, like I'd done something scandalous.

"What?" I inquired.

"We saw you go into Carol's ro-om!" Charles blurted.

laughter erupted within the crowd. Between the laughing faces, I looked at Fayola with an annoyed expression, silently asking for backup. Fayola just looked at me with a smile that told me she sided with Dante.

Rolling my eyes, I explained myself: "I went to her to ask her how magic works. That's *it*."

"Are you su-ure?" Charles teased, leaning forward with his hands still on his hips.

Once again, laughter.

"Children, all of you. Children." I replied, sarcastically. Specifically, to Charles, but I'm sure he knew that.

"Whatever," Dante replied, jokingly.

A rock of the boat startled us. Looking around, then up, we spotted Ravine in the air. Not doing anything in particular, just flying around.

"What," Paris squinted to look up at her. "You don't like us anymore?"

"Stretching!" She called down to us. "Unless any of you want a ride?"

Fayola quickly stepped forward to shut down the idea. She signed to us what Commander Woodlaine told us before: 'Don't attract any attention as we get closer to enemy waters.'

Everyone knew she was right, but everyone also wanted to know what it felt like to fly, I guess. As if most of us hadn't already been carried off by a gargoyle before.

Dante agreed with Fayola, which surprised me. He said, "Yeah, Fay's probably right. We're much closer than we were before, we shouldn't attract any trouble."

"Oh, come on," Paris nudged- probably tried to shove- Dante with her elbow. "You would have killed to fly just two days ago and now you don't want it?"

I butted in before Dante could answer. "Come on guys, we're too close to the end of this trip to be making dumb decisions. Besides, If we get caught again your asses are on the chopping block."

Fayola agreed with me, firmly.

"You're not *scared*, are you Ned?" Ravine taunted me. Charles and Paris snickered to each other. I don't know if she thought we were friends, but we definitely weren't. I refrained from making a face I shouldn't have and instead forced a laugh. Not a much better option, really.

"Scared of what?" I pushed. Looking up, I saw only a silhouette in front of bright sun rays.

"Oh, ho, ho," Ravine laughed in a deep voice. "Those are fightin' words, buddy."

As I laughed, I saw the silhouette getting bigger. Ravine was coming closer down, and fast. For a moment, I assumed she was going to land. But only for a moment. When I finally realized that she was coming at *me* like a lightning bolt, I had no time to react.

Her talons gripped my shoulders hard, and I was flung from the boat. I was trying so hard to be nice, to tolerate Ravine. I had very little reaction to her swinging me through the air. With a deep breath, I controlled my words.

"Okay Ravine, very funny, put me down," I stated, monotone.

"You don't like flying?" She teased.

"If you wanna fly with one of us so badly, fly with Paris! She actually *likes* you." I squirmed in her grip.

"She does?" Ravine said, but then she caught herself. "Well, I think all of you like me, even just a little bit."

"Why should *I* like *you*?" I scoffed at her.

"Because I'm trying to fix my mistakes, Ned! How many times do you want me to apologize?"

"You can't just fix it, Ravine. Unless you can do necromancy, you can't '*fix*' that."

"I know that but I'm doing all I can do! I've committed treason just for a chance to say sorry! I'm helping you guys! I'm-"

"Wait, stop." Throughout the conversation, Ravine's movements slowed. There was something dark in the distance, in the sky. I kept trying to get a good look at it, but she just kept moving and flinging me every which way.

"Really? I don't get a chance to explain myself. I-"

"Ravine, seriously stop moving." My tone dropped earnestly.

Finally, she stopped. "God, Ned, what. What? What is it this time?"

"What is that? In the distance over there," Ravine provided shade over me, but I still squinted to try and see any details of what it was. Whatever it was, it was getting closer. I looked down, and the group was starting to notice what I was looking at.

"I- I don't know-" Suddenly, what must've been hundreds of the same black silhouette came into view. My heart sank into my stomach. I quickly looked to my right and left; there were a few ships in the distance.

"It's gargoyles, they know we're here," I said, sounding more calm than I felt.

In no time at all Ravine and I had lowered to the deck of the ship. We hastily made our way downstairs to prepare for battle. A sword, bow, and a shield was all I had time to grab. Stepping out of my cabin, I heard General Adian's shouts and commands above me. To my right, Carol was struggling to shove on her armor. I sheathed my sword and rushed to her aid.

"What's happening?" She asked frantically, leaving me to fix her armor.

"Gargoyles spotted us, we've gotta get up there and help," I tugged at the last strap. It wouldn't budge. "C'mon, stupid thing."

Carol tugged it the other way.

It snapped into place.

"Alright then," I said.

"Let's go,"

"Let's."

We dashed up the stairs, as we were coming up Paris trailed behind us. Everyone else was most likely already on deck.

In a moment of adrenaline, I whipped open the squeaky cabin door. Before I could take in the bright sun or anything else around me, a gargoyle pummeled me into the ground. He lashed at me with his teeth and managed to barely block him by shoving my forearm against his throat, keeping his jaws just inches from my face.

Just as I was about to counterattack, a sword slashed off the head of the gargoyle on me. The head rolled away, and the body was kicked off of me. I looked up, my eyes adjusting to the sun, and General Aidan was looking down at me. Literally and figuratively.

"Uh,"

Before I could even start my sentence, Aidan stabbed the wood next to my head. If I had an ear there before, It would've been sliced off.

"I argue in you all's favor after the first time this happened and this is what you do?" He snapped.

"I-"

"Get up." He said as he pulled his sword out of the wood. He ignored me and continued to fight.

I did as ordered. My nerves spiked with fear of my consequences, but that was only if I made it out of any of this alive. At the moment, I didn't know which result I feared more.

Gargoyles came from every direction but down. Carol and Ravine took to the skies to try and keep anything they could from the ship. From the deck, Paris and Fayola shot them down using their bows when they weren't being actively attacked. I tried to protect myself and them as best I could, so they had more time to shoot.

Turning around, I saw two gargoyles tackle Dante. I jumped to action, slicing at them left and right. Finally, I stabbed one through the side of its rib and I flung it off my sword into the ocean. When I turned back around, I saw the last gargoyle on Dante's back. Before he or I could do anything, it sunk its cement teeth into his shoulder.

"Dante!" I yelled, rushing over.

He yelled in pain, but before I could get to him, he reached backwards, grabbed it by the horn and ripped it forwards off his back.

Dante's blood flung from its jaw and onto me. He threw it off the boat, farther than anyone should be able to throw anyone that size.

"Damn," I gasped. I wiped my face and rushed to Dante's side. The wound was big and deep, especially since he ripped the guy's teeth through himself. Dante was on his knee, holding his arm in place. He didn't speak but his face said enough- eyes wide and shaky breaths.

"Stay calm, you're fine," Using my dagger, I sliced his sash off of him and used it to wrap up his shoulder.

Before I could finish tying the knot a gargoyle grabbed me by my own shoulders and began to fly away with me.

Dante, with his good arm, grabbed my foot and slammed both me and the gargoyle onto the deck. My dagger was still in my hand, so before the gargoyle could get back up I sliced her achilles heel and she shrieked in pain. I stood back up but before I could get to her she retreated to the air. Wasting no time, I ran to Dante.

As I finished tying the knot that had been ripped loose, his mind appeared to be back in his head.

"Thanks," he breathed.

"Don't rip them through you, if you're gonna do that try to kill the gargoyle while they're on you and then pull the teeth out of the wound gently.

"Smart," He replied, still out of breath.

"Charles!" screamed Paris' voice behind me.

I whipped my head around and heard a splash. I wish I could go three seconds

without one of my friends being in mortal danger.

I ran to Paris and leaned so far over the edge of the boat I almost fell off myself.

That's when I saw Charles in the water, flailing helplessly. As soon as he could get up for air, a gargoyle would swoop down and either cut him, stab him, or push him back under.

Without thinking, I broke off in a sprint down the ship to the foremast. Paris stayed behind, shooting at any gargoyle that got close to him.

When I got there, I wasted no time loosening a rope and climbing to its peak. Once at the top, I took a deep breath and jumped off the post. I held onto the bottom of the rope and let it loosen and loosen until it met its end, and I jerked upwards as I unsheathed my sword. I carefully but swiftly angled myself as I shot towards the spot Charles was. I gripped my sword tight. I had one shot- once chance and-

Slice. Two pairs of wings in the ocean, their owners falling in the water along with them. As I swung past Charles, I put away my sword and got as low as I could to the sea level. Coming back around to Charles, I saw nothing but his hat bobbing in the water. I got even closer and prayed I would see him- any sign of him.

Then a hand shot up through the water. I sighed with relief and grabbed his hand, pulling him out of the water. I flung him onto the boat, and he rolled not-so-gracefully across the deck.

What I hadn't planned for was getting myself back on the boat. I took a leap of faith when I thought I was high up enough, but/the rope and the soles of my boots were wet, and I slipped. I didn't get far enough off the rope and I hit the side of the boat, hard. I hardly had enough time to grab the rail as I slid down the side of the boat.

Finally, I reached up. I extended my arm as far as I could in hopes that anyone would catch me.

Just before I would hit the water, I stopped falling. I looked back up and there was Aidan, leaning almost all the way over the rail. He managed to grab my wrist in time, and I grabbed his. He hoisted me a bit too easily over the deck and I balanced myself.

I immediately went to Charles, who lay unconscious on the deck. Paris was kneeled over him, frantically checking his pulse. The world seemed to move in slow motion as I fell to his side.

"His heart's stopped!" Paris cried.

I immediately got to work performing CPR. "Plug his wounds!" I ordered Paris hastily.

While she stopped his bleeding, I prayed. I pumped his chest as hard as I could and prayed. "C'mon, Charles, c'mon, please."

Fear and dread welled in my chest. I couldn't let him die, I just couldn't. I stopped pumping his chest and did mouth to mouth for ten seconds, then back to pumping. Paris finished plugging his wounds and held her bloody gloves over her mouth in fear. I kept pumping, even though I heard a rib snap. I noticed that anyone who wasn't actively fighting a gargoyle was surrounding Charles and I, protecting us. I just kept pumping.

I was just starting to lose hope when Charles coughed up an ungodly amount of water and blood and rolled over onto his side. I groaned in relief and folded, dropping my head onto his side and putting my hands on the back of my head, running my fingers through my hair. "Holy shit," He coughed.

"You asshole, don't do that." I began to control my breathing again.

"I think it's over. It was just a small fleet." General Aidan sighed, out of breath. "Is everyone here?"

"Everyone who stays on land is," Commander Woodlaine answered. "I dunno about the other two." Woodlaine looked to the skies.

Carol and Ravine weren't on the boat. I looked up and saw clear skies. Well, clear of gargoyles. The skies turned foggy and gray; I couldn't see ten feet into the air. Suddenly the boat jolted to a stop. We hit the docks. Ravine and Carol approached us through the fog.

"The docks are clear, there's no one in any of the shops or taverns," Carol explained.

"Not even for miles. This place is abandoned, but now even more of the area is just desolate." Ravine added.

"They must be expecting us then," Aidan responded, analyzing the docks in front of him and the abrupt weather change. It was dead quiet aside from the waves. The fog was thick but Carol's glow lit up the docks. There was snowfall- it was light but it was enough to stick.

"Alright," General Aidan stepped off the boat as the other ships got to the docks. "This is it."

Fifteen

Have A Holly, Jolly Christmas

December twenty-fifth. Christmas day. Ironically, the same day my father made his name known. I thought about this as we snuck through abandoned roads and dark alleyways. I was focused. Focused on the importance of my role in this moment. Focused on what could happen if I didn't spontaneously *get* magic. Focused on everything but General Aidan trying to get my attention.

"Cadet. Nutcracker." He snapped.

"Yes sir?" I popped back into reality.

"Merry Christmas." His tone became much lighter.

"Merry Christmas, Sir," I responded, focusing back into my surroundings.

"Whatever happens, Cadet," he stopped and turned to me. "We've got your back,"

"Thanks," I stopped too. I figured we were waiting for the rest of the group to catch up. "I just hope everything goes like it's supposed to,"

"It will." Aidan reassured me.

The rest of the group caught up with us and we continued creeping along the coast.

"Plotting are we?" Paris chuckled.

"Nope, just exchanging a Merry Christmas." Aidan responded.

Paris laughed a little, but the silence afterward was suffocating. As if they realized, 'Oh yeah, today is the day your dad killed King Micenor, isn't it? Aw man, he's dead now. And you have to kill a king today too. Or maybe you won't and become a failure. Who knows.'

"Well then. Merry Christmas, Sir." Paris finished her thought finally.

"How much farther do we have to go?" Dante asked. We fashioned him a makeshift sling out of materials we found around the market-place at the docks. We put his armor on over it as best we could, but the sling makes him a target still, like weak prey. We all have a good reason to be prey to the gargoyles.

"Another block or two, I suppose," General Aidan answered. "The neighborhoods look aristocratic; we have to be close to the Castle."

Then, Fayola grabbed General Aidan's shoulder lightly. When we turned to look at her, she had a finger over her mouth, shushing us. Her eyes pointed upwards, and she started to lower herself to the ground, as if she was hiding from something. We all lowered with her, looking to the skies to find what she saw. Not too far in the distance, I spotted the silhouette of a gargoyle in silver-colored armor on a perch.

'Must be surveillance.' Aidan signed to us. 'Follow me and stay low.'

We followed him single file against the wall of an alley. As we tip-toed by the gargoyles I prayed they didn't see us. I couldn't stop think-ing of what could go wrong. What would happen if they saw us now? Could they kill us? How would the war end? Would it end at all?

Charles quietly punched me in the shoulder. He pointed to my forehead and mouthed to me 'Stop overthinking, you're gonna be fine.' I swallowed my worries and kept after General Aidan.

After a bit more creeping, General Aidan whispered to us that we were past the guards.

"Those were castle guards, we're past the front gates. We just have to get around the courtyard to the throne room."

A chill went down my spine. It reminded me of my king: large, strong, sturdy. I imagined if all of that wanted to kill me. Surely their king isn't actually in the throne room, right? Surely, they took him somewhere safe?

Aidan stopped. "We're here."

The ground began to rumble. Distant yelling of gargoyles and neighing of horses grew louder and louder.

This caught all of our attention and immediately put us on edge. Swords were unsheathed and bows were drawn. And then, all at once, two of our horses raced around a corner about half a block to our right. Commander Woodlaine was on one of the horses, and Ravine followed close behind, trying to hold off the gargoyle soldiers that followed. The swarm was hot on their tail.

"Woodlaine!" General Aidan shouted, firing his arrow at the mass of gargoyles behind Commander Woodlaine.

This triggered arrows to fly from all of our bows. Just when we thought we'd gotten most of them down, more seemed to tunnel through.

Woodlaine arrived quickly on their horse, the other one trailing close behind. As soon as they did, General Aidan jumped and swung himself onto the horse's back with ease. We drew our swords as Ravine continued to fight them off. General Aidan and Commander Woodlaine's horses began to kick down the door to the throne room. We slashed and swung and shot and stabbed relentlessly at the mob of gray, and then, almost just as soon as they arrived, something happened.

Carol stood in front of us, as we stood around Aidan and Woodlaine on their horses. a shield of green fire disintegrated any gargoyle that dared to touch it. General Aidan and Commander Woodlaine took this opportunity to bash the gate in. Both of them commanded their horses to kick the door down. But someone was missing.

"Carol! Carol!" Ravine's voice barely echoed behind the dome of fire that surrounded us. "Let me in! Please!" She pleaded.

Carol was struggling to hold all the gargoyles back. But she managed to pull a small hole near the back of the dome, near the gate into the throne room. Ravine tumbled through, bringing with her a couple of gargoyles. They tugged and gnawed at her wings and shouted profanities at her, calling her a traitor and disloyal. They called her weak and useless- a failure. The puppeteered gargoyle soldiers only said things that they were commanded to say by King Khelbent.

Ravine roared a deep, guttural screech as she flapped her wings backwards, smacking the gargoyles off of her wings. She threw a small ornament at them, and it blew up the gargoyles with glass and purple flames.

The ornament, though, also blew a hole in the top of the flame. The purple flames spread through Carol's green and gold shield for just a moment. But a moment was all one gargoyle needed.

Just as General Aidan and Commander Woodlaine finally kicked in the gate, the gargoyle shot in the ring of purple flames and grabbed Commander Woodlaine by the shoulders and flew them through the gate swiftly.

Aidan reached up to try and grab them, but he missed just by a hair. It flew off with Woodlaine, who was struggling to reach the dagger in their sheath. Instantaneously, General Aidan whipped around on his horse and sped through the courtyard and into the throne room, following where the gargoyle was taking Commander Woodlaine. Charles, and myself - followed him while Fayola, Dante, and Paris stayed at the gate - Paris tending to Ravine and Fayola, and Dante trying to keep the gargoyles outside Carol's shield at bay.

We didn't get very far into the throne room before we saw him.

King Khelbent.

He was even bigger and more monstrous than I first imagined- he was even bigger than King Klaus. He looked as if he was chiseled from obsidian, unlike any other gargoyle I'd ever seen. There were cracks running up and through his shiny outer layer. I could only see so much through his armor, but I could see his horrible face. He had a strong, pronounced chin and horns longer than my arm. They twisted and turned forward in a sharp, striking pattern. His eyes glowed a deep orange and red, as if there was lava bubbling behind his face. His expression was stern, but not scared. No, he looked expectant.

He was here the whole time we fought.

He was here, waiting for us.

Worst of all, we found Commander Woodlaine in his grasp. They looked more angry than scared, but they struggled against his grasp all the same.

"Stay behind me, you two." General Aidan adjusted his horse to stand in front of Charles and I.

The roar of Carol's shield died down to a crackle. I looked over and saw Fayola, Dante, Paris, and Ravine sneaking around the wall, out of King Khelbent's view. Carol retreated, with Commander Woodlaine's horse, to where I was. She stood adjacently behind me, with the horse on her other side. Charles stood directly next to me on the other side.

It was so quiet you could hear a pin drop. The air was still, with snowflakes and specks of dust floating in the air. The castle looked like ruins of gray stones and obsidian that reflected the sunlight. A red carpet trailed all the way to the throne that King Khelbent sat on. The throne itself was made out of glossy obsidian and rubies.

King Khelbent began to speak. But, before he could, I heard the stretching of a bow. We looked around, and on top of the courtyard wall, I saw Fayola with her bow drawn, aimed at King Khelbent. Dante stood next to her with his sword drawn. On the other side, Ravine stood with Paris. Ravine held two ornament-bombs and Paris had her bow drawn.

Finally, he spoke.

"There is no reason to fight, General," King Khelbent adjusted his grip on Commander Woodlaine. "That is not why I am here."

"Then why are you fighting?" General Aidan asked, calmly. He stared sharply through King Khelbent.

"All I want," King Khelbent redirected his stare. "Is her."

He was looking at Carol. I didn't break my glare at the king, but I reached back slightly for Carol's hand. She reached for my hand too.

"You'll never have her power. Not over my dead body." General Aidan stated. I couldn't tell if he was putting up a brave front or if he was really just that brave. In the moment, both of those options felt spectacularly brave.

"Allow me to put it in a way you might understand better." King Khelbent extended his empty hand and pulled Commander Woodlaine closer to himself. "Give me the girl, or your Commander dies."

General Aidan tightened his grip on his sword, not saying anything.

"Are you saying, General, that you'd not give up one victory, one more mark on your almost perfect record, to save the one who looks up to you?"

General Aidan clenched his jaw. "Almost perfect?"

"Well, I wouldn't call your greatest hero dying under your advisory a victory, especially since his only son was placed under your care." He spoke slowly and intently. His deep, monstrous voice carried through the throne room like a tree falling in the woods. "And don't think that I'm unaware of your mistakes as the leader of your old Cadet Team, General."

I took a few steps forward, but Carol tugged me back slightly. "You know *nothing* about my father's death! *Nothing!*"

Much to my surprise, Charles joined in. "General Navid's name will be remembered and praised! Yours will be forgotten and left in the rubble and ruin of your castle!"

There was silence for a moment after that. But General Aidan started to speak.

"You will not disrespect Navid Nutcracker's name in my presence."

"I will do whatever I please." King Khelbent tightened his grip on Commander Woodlaine. I could tell he was starting to get impatient.

"I am growing tired of your defiance. This is your last chance to end this civilly, General Aidan Ambercory. Hand over-" He emphasized, "-The girl."

Before General Adian could retort, Carol stepped in front of Aidan and I.

"Let him have me," Carol looked up to General Aidan, tears welling in her eyes. "He could never make me fight for him."

"No!" I cut in instantly. "Don't do this, Carol, please! He'll just kill you if you don't do what he wants." I begged her, lowering my voice next to her. I disobeyed orders again walking next to her.

"I don't care," Carol's voice broke and a tear rolled down her cheek. "I refuse to let you all die just because of me."

"No one's gonna die, just wait. Please, just wait." I held Carol by the arm. I couldn't find the words to say in that moment.

Aidan started to say something, but then:

"Don't listen to her Aidan!" Woodlaine screamed from across the throne room.

We all turned to their direction.

"We both know she is infinitely more important to our future than I am!"

"Auden," General Aidan started shakily, but was quickly interrupted.

"No, Aidan! Please don't sacrifice anyone else's future just for me! A world where this war is lost for our people is not one I want to live in! Let me go!" Commander Auden Woodlaine screamed. Tears started to stream down their face. Their breathing was deep and wheezy, any of us could tell that King Khelbent was crushing their lungs.

"He's punctured everything inside me, I won't make it home anyways Aidan, please," they cried again, coughing. "Let me go."

General Aidan lowered from his horse. "No, no!" I could tell he was scared. His face didn't show his fear, but I could practically see his thoughts- he was looking for a solution.

There wasn't one.

"I will *not* wait for you any longer! You had two chances to save your friend!" King Khelbent tightened his fist even harder until a loud snap echoed through the throne room. Commander Woodlaine let out a final scream as he flung them to the side, hitting the wall as if he'd thrown a doll across the room.

"NO!" Aidan yelled in agony as if he had been the one thrown across the room. I'd never heard him yell so loudly, with so much hurt. Aidan ran to Woodlaine's side, lowering to his knees next to them. All any of us could do was just watch. He grabbed their wrist and shakily put his thumb against it- checking for a pulse. Words couldn't describe the look on King Khelbent's face as he watched Adian hold Woodlaine.

Aidan rose back up quickly, and yelled the most rageful, excruciating war cry I'd ever even hoped to hear in my entire life. In a second, he unsheathed his sword and was charging King Khelbent. I started off in a sprint with him, unsheathing my sword in the process. I could hear Carol's and Charles' footsteps pacing behind me. I could hear Carol crying.

"Do you see your handiwork, General? And Ravine, my sweet, *disloyal* Ravine, is this what you hoped to achieve when you left your home at the castle? Is this the ideal future you had in mind?" King Khelbent taunted.

"I am *not* loyal to torturers and murderers!" Ravine screamed from the tower as she fought off other gargoyle soldiers. "And this is *not* my home!"

As General Adian reached the throne, King Khelbent unsheathed his own colossal sword and unleashed its full weight onto Aidan with a powerful blow.

Aidan parried the swing just barely. With a spin, Aidan began to drag his sword through the front of King Khelbent's forearm. The king let out a deep outcry.

I made it to the throne where King Khelbent now stood in all his ugly glory. He had to be at *least* twice as tall as I am.

I jumped and raised my sword to gain leverage.

I brought my sword down as hard as I could onto his shoulder. Thanks to Aidan and I's efforts, King Khelbent's right arm was defective.

After myself came Charles. After King Khelbent's failed left-hand reach at my sword, he continued turning to grab Charles on my left. He slid just under the king's grasp and sliced through his shin. The King fell to his knees, but the fight wasn't over yet.

But then, in a fit of rage, King Khelbent swung his arm back around and flung Aidan and me back several feet. The back of my head hit the ground first, then I bounced and rolled even farther back. I couldn't tell how Aidan landed but I couldn't hear him.

I looked up in time to see King Khelbent reaching behind him for Charles.

"Charles!" I yelled, with what little strength I could muster.

Charles scrambled to get out of the king's reach, but just before he would've been grabbed, Ravine swooped down and scooped him up with her talons. She tossed him out of the way and he rolled, rather gracefully, in my direction. The world had started to spin in the moment, but I could see that Ravine and Carol had taken over the fight. I could hear the whistle of arrows raining down on King Khelbent from above.

As I lay on the ground, half conscious, I remembered training with Charles as a child. He always was the more acrobatic one, wasn't he?

"Ned!" Charles said, with worry flooding his eyes. "Ned get up, are you okay?" Charles helped me up and I shook away the pain as best I could.

Now would be a really great time to get magic, I thought to myself.

"Ned talk to me, are you okay?" He put his hand on the back of my head, and it stung. When he pulled his hand back, there was blood on his gloves.

"I'm okay, where's General Adian?" I asked.

"Right here," Aidan groaned, limping toward Charles and I.

'Oh God,' I thought. 'he's hurt,'

I looked down and saw a huge gash running down the side of his leg. Both Charles and I gasped in shock.

"Oh, my God, Aidan!" Charles yelled. "Your leg!"

"I'll be fine," Aidan gritted his teeth. "It's up to you now, Ned." He took a step closer and put his arm on my shoulder, using me for balance. A streak of blood ran down his face.

Carol's screams disrupted the moment. We whipped our heads around to see her and Ravine in his grasp. He dropped Ravine at his side, and her wings crumbled to bits as she collapsed next to the throne.

Carol's magic started to implode on herself- the more she struggled the more her magic built up around her.

"Carol!" I dashed towards her, the fog in my head dissipating in an instant. My sword was already drawn- I just needed to swing. I thrust my sword toward the King's chest.

He parried it.

Back and forth and back and forth we swung and heaved our swords at each other. I didn't know how long I could keep it up. My eyes darted around in search of assistance from my team. Ravine was too weak to fight. Carol was being held against her own magic. Fayola and Dante were fighting off hordes of gargoyles. Paris was struggling to hold her own against the mob of gargoyles on her side.

I let my guard down for too long. The king swung, and I blocked it just in time with my sword. His blade was just inches from my face, pushing closer.

I thought about my team. I knew Fayola and Dante had each other, but Paris was all by herself. "Charles, go help Paris!" I yelled without looking back at him. I could only assume he was tending to General Aidan's wound at the time.

It really was up to me now.

The pressure was still on me and my sword. It started to cut through the metal. If I tried to move, King Khelbent's sword would crush me instantly. I tried to think of anything, anything at all that I could do to save myself.

But before I could move myself, a gargoyle slammed me into the dirt face first. It hit me like a truck, yet before I could process that pain the King's sword pushed straight through my abdomen into the dirt below me. I screamed out in pain, my head was throbbing, I couldn't move. All I could do was look up and see Paris being detained and held down by a hoard of gargoyles atop the wall. I could see Adian propped up against the base of the wall, his leg wrapped in some makeshift cloth. And then I saw Charles sprinting towards me. My vision was blurry, but I could see the shine of tears in his eyes. With my ear pressed against the dirt, I could barely hear his yells.

Charles drew his sword and fought. I'd never seen him swing a sword so ruthlessly. He managed to kill several gargoyles that attacked the two of us. But alas, there were too many of them for Charles to fight on his own. They threw both of our swords to the side, far out of reach. Charles struggled against their hold relentlessly. I could feel myself fading, bleeding out.

Nevertheless, I pushed against the dirt, using all the strength I had left in me. I coughed up some blood, and with my head off the ground I could hear Charles' screams and Carol's cries better. I looked back over to the wall. Aidan was limping over to our swords as fast as he could. He managed to reach them and hold off quite a few gargoyles before they abused his leg injury and pinned him down. Even with one leg down, General Aidan fought better and with more class than any of the rest of us could fight with two legs.

My arms were shaking. They couldn't hold me up. I began to prop myself up on my knee, but the gargoyles kicked me back over.

So much for it being up to me. For being the chosen one. So much for magic.

They kicked and stabbed and punched and berated. They whipped and stabbed and pushed and scratched. They beat me until I couldn't even think.

In the midst of all this, I managed to turn my head against the fists of the gargoyles to the other side and look up using only my eyes. One gargoyle kicked into the open stab wound that ran across my abdomen. I curled in on myself in pain. Again, I looked up. I saw Carol crying, screaming, struggling. I thought she was trying to escape. But the magic around her looked different. The magic was going *into* King Khelbent. I thought at first that she was screaming at me, but after a closer look I realized she was screaming in pain. He was *hurting* her.

I was angry, beyond rational thought. I wanted to save her, but I couldn't. I grunted and pushed as hard as I could, but they dragged me back. I could hardly lift my hand to my sheath- but everything was gone anyways. No dagger, no bow, no arrows, no sword, nothing. Not even a pin or a pocketknife.

I gave up. I didn't have a choice. I let my head drop to the ground. The soil was soft, and cool. I just wanted to die already so I didn't have to watch everything I'd ever loved die.

That's when I heard Charles' scream.

"Nedrall Nutcracker, don't you dare give up on us! Don't you dare even think about it! We've fought for you! Since the day we first signed up for this shit I've been here for *you*! Since the day you met Fay and Dante and Paris! Since the day your father died! Since the day Aidan gave us our first training session! Since the day that Ravine decided to help us! Since the day Carol first saved you in the woods! *That's* what we're all here for, Ned! *We* didn't give up on you so don't you *dare* give up on us!"

Dammit.

This whole time I was so worried about what people wanted me to do for everyone else that I couldn't see what everyone else was doing for me. Everything led up to this moment, right now.

"Ned!" General Aidan yelled across the courtyard to me while he was pinned down. "Give him hell!"

"Get up, Ned!" Paris screamed.

"Go, Ned! Go!" Dante joined in the screaming.

I looked over at Dante and Fayola. They had about seven gargoyles holding each of them. I looked at Fayola- she looked into my eyes, sternly, like a mother's. She didn't break eye contact through the punching and beating. As if she was telling me to get up and fight.

"Ned heads up!" Ravine yelled to me from behind the throne. I looked toward the throne and saw an ornament flying towards me. I braced for impact, but instead of hitting me, the ornament hit the ground behind me.

All of the gargoyles around me were blown up and away. The blast pushed and rolled me towards the throne.

Now was my only chance.

I struggled to stand, and the king looked at me pitifully. Aidan threw his sword to me. I picked it up and looked at King Khelbent with disdain.

I could tell that Carol was in pain, trying to keep her magic inward.

"How 'bout that?" I told the king. If I was going to die, I won't give him the satisfaction of my fear.

"Every second you aren't killing me, I'm getting stronger and your precious Christmas Spirit is getting weaker," King Khelbent boasted.

"Then I guess I should kill you," I said, reeling back my sword.

He swung his sword at me, and I parried it. I thrust my sword at his arm. It sliced his finger. He waited for me to swing again, as if he wanted me to attack him. I was still horribly wounded, but I couldn't give up now.

He swung, I parried.

I swung, I missed.

It was a pathetic back and forth of fencing. For him, it must've been like fighting an inexperienced child.

I swung, I missed.

He swung, but I couldn't dodge in time.. With one swift blow, he sliced my hand clean off. It, with my sword, fell to the ground. I grabbed my wrist, writhing in pain. I dropped to one knee. But, I gritted my teeth and reached for my sword with my other hand.

As I reached for my sword, I heard a swift *schlink* and felt a hot pain rip through my chest.

I dangled off the edge of the sword as he raised me up, level to his face. I could feel my heart slowing and my breaths getting heavier. Blood poured out of my chest and my mouth onto the ground below me. With my hand occupied, I tried to use my forearms to keep his sword from splitting me in half. If this kept up I'd lose both my hands.

Carol screamed my name. The magic swirling around her looked like an angry spinning cocoon of fire. It seeped into King Khelbent's arm, and I could feel the power coming through his sword.

The sphere of her magic was in reach, but it would probably hurt like hell to touch it. It might even kill me. But there was something I had to try.

With my sword in my hand, I reached it across my body, poking the end of the sword into Carol's magic swirl of flames. I thought it would explode, but it didn't. It started doing something different.

The instant the metal touched the flames, they spiraled up my sword, up my arm and around my whole body. The flames engulfed me, but they didn't hurt me. Instead, I could breathe again. I could feel my blood circulating my body with every beat of my heart. The pain began to slowly disappear. I reached my right arm forward where I could see it, and I saw my hand grow back the way it was before.

Well, not exactly the way it was before.

My hand was made of wood. I could move it and feel the wind blowing against it all the same, but it was rough like tree bark. I looked down at my wounds- all of them filled themselves in with wood. Every cut, stab, and scrape- all of it healed with wood in its place. A few cuts sprouted leaves. As I observed all the healing that was happening, I noticed something in my boots. They were also turning to wood, and suddenly the hope and excitement of healing turned to dread again.

And then the fire was gone, and so were the gargoyles, and I dropped back onto the ground.

I looked at my feet, at that point the wood was up my shins.

I immediately looked at King Khelbent. His sword wasn't in me anymore- there was instead a branchy-green replica.

I charged, with not one thought except hope. Hope that I could end this once and for all.

The wood was spreading faster and faster up my body. As I was rapidly approaching the throne, my knees had been locked into place.

I got to the throne, and I was almost half-statue.

I took a leap of faith.

I brought my sword down through King Khelbent's shoulder like an evergreen hellfire. My blade ran down his chest, through his heart, and finally sliced him in half as I landed on the ground in front of the throne. I could feel that something new had awakened in me, it felt like a new life. Dad was right, like he always was.

As the wooden infection rose up my chest like high water, I saw that I'd done it. I'd killed the king of gargoyles and ended the war.

I knew what was happening to me, but I didn't know if it could be reversed. So, in my final moment of peace, I looked up at the sky. If only my dad could see me now.

Sixteen

Oh My God Is He Dead?

I was still there. Somehow. I couldn't move, not even my eyes. I stared into the sun that began to peek from behind the clouds, but my eyes didn't burn. I started to realize I couldn't feel anything. Not physically, at least. I started to panic, but I was disrupted by Carol's sobbing. She was screaming and crying, asking what she had done, that it was all her fault.

I wanted to tell her that everything was okay. I wanted to tell her that I was alive and I could hear her. But I couldn't. I could feel my feet rooting themselves into the ground through the cracks of the cobblestone below me.

Carol hung on me, cursing and crying and holding me. But then, I felt a different hand on my back. I couldn't tell who it was, I couldn't hear them, and I couldn't see anything but the sun.

My heart sank when I heard his voice, though. "Ned?" It was Charles. "What happened? What's this?" His voice was shaky and light. I didn't want to leave either of them yet. I wasn't ready.

Charles moved his arms around my waist in a hug, burying his face in my back. He sobbed hysterically, repeating "No, no, no."

I heard hard footsteps hit the ground. Must've been Dante, Paris, and Fay landing.

"What happened?" Seemed to be the common question among all of them. Carol told them that she didn't know what happened or how it did, only that she was trying to keep me alive.

I wanted to scream out so bad that I was there. Instead, I got to stare into the sun as all of my friends cried and held me.

Eventually, I saw Fayola's face. Of course, she was a head and a half taller than me. She just held my face in her hand.

"We have to go back," Ravine said. Her voice, like the others, was tearful. "We have to tell the others that it's over."

"What do we do with Ned?" Charles snapped. "We can't just leave him here."

"Is there any way to turn him back?" I heard Aidan's fearful voice from behind me.

"*No*," Carol sobbed. "I've never been able to change anybody back to normal before, I don't know how."

Every emotion raced through me at once. The only noise I could hear was people crying. There was nothing I could do but sit in my panic and fear and regret. It didn't feel real. But I knew that even if I was stuck like this forever, I was still here; the war was over, and everyone could go home.

As the sun continued to shine, I could hear my team comforting each other. I was glad they still had each other.

"We have to tell the others that it's over." Aidan spoke, and I assumed it was his hand that was placed on my shoulder. "I need you all to come with me. Carol, do you think you can get him out of the ground?" Aidan's voice held a gentleness and sadness I'd never thought possible from him.

"I'll try," Carol said through sniffs. "Just give me a minute."

I heard sniffles and footsteps get quieter, and then the mounting of horses. The gallops of horses grew quieter, and then the only thing I heard were Carol's soft sobs.

"Nedrall? She whispered, "Are you there?"

Yes, yes, please find a way to fix this, please, I'm here. But it was only a thought.

"I want to believe you are." She levitated slightly and entered my view. I could no longer see the sun, but I saw mine.

"Can you see me?" She asked. Her face was pink, and her eyelashes were wet. I thought about all the times I felt hate before that moment, and realized I hated nothing more than seeing her cry.

She pressed her forehead against mine, and the tips of our noses touched. I felt her hold the sides of my head. She cried onto me. Her tears fell onto my eyes and cheeks, they ran down the sides of my face past her hands and around my chin, falling from there onto my boots.

"I love you," She whispered to me. I wanted to say it back so desperately. I wanted it so bad that I thought maybe a tear might well in my wooden eye, but I knew that couldn't happen.

She leaned in closer and kissed me. She kissed me for a long time, and I thought, *if there was one thing I could do right now, and then go back to being a statue forever, it would be to kiss you right now.*

She ended the kiss, but still held my face. She looked into my eyes, then up near the top of my head.

She gasped, wide-eyed. She immediately ran her fingers through my hair.

My first thought when I felt this was '*What?*' Which, at the time, felt like an appropriate response for someone running their hands through hair that was supposedly wooden.

"Ned!" She exclaimed, a smile spreading from ear to ear on her beautiful face.

I felt my nose again, I inhaled sharply. Suddenly the dusty, dark air of the ruined castle was the freshest air I'd ever breathed in my life.

Before I knew it, I could control my whole head. The answer was right here in front of us the whole time: if she turned living beings into trees out of fear, then surely she could turn them back out of love!

"Carol? *Carol!*" I burst out with laughter. "Oh my God!" It almost didn't feel real, the second chance at life.

I could move my arms again, and I hugged her. I held her head close to my chest. She hugged me back for a moment, then pushed off of me, and looked into my eyes. This time I didn't see tears; I just saw her grin.

I brought her head close to mine, gently. I closed my eyes and kissed her, and I knew at that moment that this is what I'd been fighting for. For this moment, this universally perfect moment. I wanted that kiss to last forever, and for a moment it did. It lasted until I could feel my feet again. That's when I broke the kiss and twirled her in my arms, holding her close again.

When I stopped spinning, I was facing the gate rather than the throne.

I saw a white horse trotting across the gate, and a black one following it. I looked to where I last saw Commander Woodlaine, and noticed that they were gone. It comforted me knowing their sacrifice didn't go to waste.

In the distance, I saw someone slip off the horse quickly and sprint at me, and the person controlling the reins of the horse got off not so quickly.

Charles and Aidan!

Carol let go of me, as she saw them too.

I broke into a sprint towards Charles. He yelled across the field.

"What the hell?" He yelled at me as we approached each other, rather quickly.

"I don't know!" I yelled back. "Magic I guess!"

We then promptly slammed into each other, but our momentum spun into a hug.

When we let go of each other, all we could do was laugh for a long time.

"What the fuck, Ned? I thought you were a tree!" he asked, placing his hands on my arms and shaking them.

"I dunno, she kissed me," I said, trying to offer up any reason for what the hell was going on.

"True love's kiss! Oh my God you're like a princess!" He cheered. He punched his fists into the air and I couldn't help but laugh, knowing that I almost missed the opportunity to laugh with my friends again.

"Congratulations, Cadet." General Adian limped up to me from behind Charles, seemingly appearing out of nowhere.

My face went red. "Uhm- thanks."

He just laughed.

We laughed with him, rather awkwardly.

Suddenly, from the gate, I heard Paris yell. "Is that Ned?"

"Oh my God Ned's alive and not a tree!" Dante yelled in response.

I looked around Aidan to see the rest of my friends running over, waving at me. Their silhouettes were thin as they approached me, but I saw all of them nonetheless. Even the minute details- like Paris and Ravine's hand-holding and Dante jumping and waving at the same time, and Fayola signing for him to stop, and I could only assume it was because of his shoulder because of her trying to tie his makeshift sling as they ran.

When they got here, I was bombarded in hugs. I could even feel the warmth radiating from Carol as she joined in the hug.

"*Ugh*, Let's go home," I said, regaining the soreness from my wounds.

"What's wrong with your hand?" Dante demanded.

I looked down at it, noticing that it remained wooden. Peering through the rips in my uniform and armor, I noticed that the wounds were also wooden. "Oh, I dunno."

"That's classic Nutcracker magic right there." Aidan laughed.

"What will happen now?" Paris asked, looking at Aidan.

Aidan took a deep breath. "We go home. The war's over."

Ravine spoke up. "My brothers were in command of the puppets, but they all have surrendered. I will try my best to rebuild this kingdom and deal with my brothers."

"I'm sure King Klaus will be forgiving of your brothers, Ravine." Aidan assured her.

"I hope so. They were misguided by my father the same way I was." Ravine looked at the throne.

"I'm sorry it had to end this way, Ravine." I apologized. "A part of me was hoping he'd surrender."

Ravine replied sharply. "Don't be, he was long overdue for his death. There was never a chance that he'd surrender."

Fayola started to sign: 'I'm just glad that we are all safe. The future is waiting for us back home.'

"I agree," Dante pitched in. "Let's go home."

The air was still and light as we walked back to Aidan and Wood-laine's horses.

Charles turned and playfully punched me in the arm. "You may be some magic hot-shot now, but to me, you'll still always be the kid who decided to venture into an enchanted forest to find a ghost he had a crush on."

"She's not a ghost, she's right here." I pulled Carol closer to me. "And I *did* find her, thank you very much."

"Look at you go, Ned." Carol giggled. "Finding the Christmas Spirit."

Megan Parker was born in Smyrna, Tennessee, and raised in Murfreesboro, Tennessee. Starting at the age of 13 in 2019, she wrote and worked on *The Gargoyle, The Nutcracker, & The Christmas Spirit* until she finished it at the age of 16.

Megan Parker has always been a creator. She loves to create short stories, Megan longs to create an experience that people could enjoy, to create a narrative journey that offers the joys of feeling connected to a story and its characters.

Megan loves to listen to music, especially while she writes. When she's not writing, Megan can be found on a soccer field or out shopping with her friends and family.

Epilogue

I woke up. It had been twenty-two days after the end of the war. Coming from where I could only assume was the kitchen, I could smell muffins. Or what was probably meant to be muffins.

Since we got back home, Carol had taken on a new hobby of cooking. It wasn't going very well. Nevertheless, I closed my eyes, inhaled deeply, and prepared to eat the twenty-second burnt breakfast in a row.

I left our room and walked groggily into the kitchen, rubbing my eyes. The scent of blueberries, sugar, and smoke filled the air. The morning sun beamed through the kitchen, and that along with Carol's glow made seeing a challenge.

"Goodmorning, love!" She said, excitedly. She was wearing one of her new dresses I'd bought her, as well as the oven mitts neither my dad nor I had touched since I left to enlist.

"Goodmorning, Sunshine," I responded, leaning on the wall. "What'cha doin'?"

"Well," She started. "Since the war ended, we'll have more time to spend in the city and not on base. Which means I have a lot of shopping to do."

"Mhm?" I listened on, sleepily.

"*And,* Ravine is being crowned Queen of Gargoyles now. She claimed the role and her brothers didn't argue with her, it seems." She said, taking black muffins out of the oven.

"Does that make Paris a princess or something?" I asked.

"I think so?" Carol stared quizzically. "I'm not sure how that works."

"I dunno either." I squeezed my eyelids together a few times to push out the tiredness. "Have you decided whether you'll stay in the Work-force or not?"

"I have." Carol straightened her shoulders. "I am going to stay. You guys are my team now, my friends, I want to stay close to you all."

"I'm sure everything will go smoother now that we're the King's guards." I said.

"I agree." Carol put down the hot muffin tray on the counter. "What's everyone else doing now?"

"Fay and Dante are helping Ravine with their farm's harvest. They're giving it out to gargoyles and soldiers who need it." I answered. Fayola and Dante were going to continue to live in the capitol, but the Generals and the King granted everyone time with their families after the war.

"Charles isn't helping them on the farm?" Carol asked with a giggle.

I laughed with her. "No way. I think Charles would rather wear those stupid uniform caps than do any kind of work on a farm."

"Well," Carol poked into one of the charred muffins disappointedly. "What is he doing lately?"

"He and Paris are working with General Codagh on a technological advancements program in the workforce."

Carol sighed. "Ah, finally putting their brilliant minds to work now that they have the time."

It's true, Charles and Paris are too smart to only be in the T.O.Y. Workforce. Charles has followed me wherever I've gone since we were kids, and when I enlisted for the workforce, it was no different. As for Paris? Well, knowing Paris, she probably joined to spite someone, as she does many things.

"What has Aidan been doing, do you know?" I hadn't been in touch with him for almost a week, since he's been busy helping the King situate the future with the other Generals.

"You know him, always keeping busy. He's trying to work with King Klaus and Ravine to figure out what to do with the gargoyle citizens and create a memorial."

"He's making a memorial?" I pried my eyes away from the black blueberry muffins to Carol.

"Yes, but more like a museum." Carol corrected. "We're all going to be in it. Our team, the Generals, and the Commanders, including Woodlaine and your father."

"Especially Woodlaine." I repeated.

Carol removed her oven mitts. "We'll be here to support Aidan if he needs it."

"That's what teams do." I sat up straight, preparing myself to brave the unknown flavor of the muffins.

"Couldn't have done it without each other, could we?" Carol leaned over the muffins towards me, her own nose scrunching at the smell reflexively.

"No, we couldn't." I really, truly understood that now. And I'm sure my team and Charles were especially thankful for it. I sure was thankful for it, too. I am alive now, thanks to Carol. I kept pushing, thanks to Charles. I kept learning, thanks to Paris, Dante, Fayola, Aidan, and my father. And thanks to Ravine, I learned how to forgive.

It took too much time to learn, but I realized I couldn't save my kingdom or anyone else before letting myself be saved first.